Her senses became suddenly more acute as her body weakened. She could feel the cold, damp mist chilling her skin and hear the sound of her heart thudding wildly against her ribs; his odor was pungent and sharp in her nostrils, and the taste of fear rose in her throat, acrid and bitter as bile. The knife moved closer to her face, held now by a disembodied hand. On the cutting edge she could see a dark stain gleaming wetly, and she knew the blood was Rena's— knew, too, that the scream rising in her throat would never be uttered. After all, who was there to hear? But she heard it in her head, the scream, high and sharp and rising, and it went on and on and became the sound of a siren, shrill and piercing, but she knew it would be too late . . .

CUTTING EDGE

CUTTING EDGE

Lisbeth Chance

A TOM DOHERTY ASSOCIATES BOOK

CUTTING EDGE

Copyright © 1985 by Lisbeth L. Chance

Reprinted by arrangement with Walker and Company

First TOR printing: June 1986

A TOR Book

Published by Tom Doherty Associates
49 West 24 Street
New York, N.Y. 10010

ISBN: 0-812-50130-6
CAN. ED.: 0-812-50131-4

Library of Congress Catalog Card Number: 84-19661

Printed in the United States of America

0 9 8 7 6 5 4 3 2 1

For K,
who didn't let me give up

Prologue

SHE LAY IN bed, fully clothed, listening.

The noise was faint, barely discernible in any other circumstances and to any other ears. But to senses already so heightened, it had the impact of a gunshot.

Her heart pounded fiercely; and her body shook with each thud, her head filled with the sound of blood pumping through her veins. A black fog that had nothing to do with the nearly total darkness swam before her eyes. Fear gripped her with devastating intensity, threatening to overwhelm reason with blind panic.

More than anything, she wanted to flee the menacing stillness of the huge house and run screaming onto the grounds, but she retained just enough self-control to realize that, if she stayed inside, she would have the advantage. Besides, running away would defeat the whole purpose of her being in this situation in the first place; he had to be caught, and she was the bait.

She drew a deep breath. *The police are here,* she reminded herself. *I'm safe, protected.* She knew the men and trusted them. They were professionals, well trained for this type of work.

They're outside, watching, she thought, *and they can hear me when I speak. Everything will be fine.* Nervously she fingered the small transmitter concealed beneath the cowl neck of her sweater. *Should I say something?* she wondered. *If he's here, if the police missed seeing him when he came in, he could be close enough to hear me. But if they did miss him, they should know . . .*

To say or not to say . . . She knew she was on the brink of hysteria and fought the impulse to laugh aloud. *This is ridiculous,* she thought, jumping at every little sound, afraid to make a simple decision.

Though the second-floor master bedroom was thick with darkness, she knew she could find her way into the bathroom without turning on a light. So she slid out of bed, pausing once to listen intently to the silence, then moved noiselessly across the plush carpet to the bathroom door.

Once again, a faintly audible sound reached her, something like fabric brushing against a smooth, solid surface. Quickly she closed the door behind her, careful to turn the knob as quietly as possible.

"I just heard something," she said, almost whispering into the tiny transmitter. "A noise downstairs, then another. It sounded close." Her voice broke. This was too much to bear alone. There were fourteen rooms in this damned house, and he could be hiding in any one of them. Why had she agreed to this insane scheme? Why couldn't someone at least have stayed here with her?

But she knew why. The psychological profile worked up by the police psychiatrist indicated that this man was unusually clever, alert, and perceptive. There was no way of knowing how closely he might be watching her; trying to conceal another person in the house was just too risky. He had to think she was completely alone and defenseless, or else he would simply wait until another time to come after her.

Besides, it was too late to back out now. With each passing second she became more and more convinced that he was in the house with her, stalking her in the darkness. All she could do was trust the police to know what they were doing.

"I think he's here, guys," she murmured. "Sure wish you could tell me what to do now." To her ears, her voice sounded surprisingly steady in view of the fact that she was trembling from head to toe.

For several long minutes, she stood completely motionless, her ear pressed against the door's paneling. She heard nothing more, but still the conviction grew that she was not alone.

Quite suddenly a picture flashed into her mind: a man, dressed in dark clothing, stealthily feeling his way along the upstairs hallway, pausing at the door to the guest room. The image was extraordinarily clear, the scene seeming to be lit by a long-burning match that illuminated the man while letting the edges of the picture blur into indistinctness. *Am I having a flash,* she thought desperately, *or is it just nervous imagination?* Not for the first time, she wished her extra sense came equipped with a bell or an indicator light.

She decided to act on the message, no matter how faulty it might be. She would assume that he was here, that the police hadn't seen him enter, and that possibly they hadn't heard her guarded whisper. The best alternative, it seemed, was to alert them in the quickest, loudest way possible. With luck, she would have enough time to get to the window, open it, and scream.

Now that she had decided to act, she was unaccountably calm. She opened the door and crept out, not pausing to listen. It wouldn't matter what she heard now; she *knew* he was here. He wanted to kill her. She had to get help.

The window was a rectangular patch of lighter darkness. Had she locked it? She didn't remember. What if it stuck? What if he materialized suddenly, blocking out even that faint patch of light?

He did.

She hadn't seen him approach; she had heard nothing. He was just there, the mass of his body nothing more than a black shadow against the backdrop of the window. She screamed.

Before the sound could be more than partially uttered, his hand was on her throat, squeezing cruelly and painfully, his thumb digging into the sensitive artery beneath her ear. He waved his other hand in front of her face; she heard a faint click and knew without doubt what he held. He had used the knife once before; she knew what unspeakable things the weapon could do in his hands.

A surge of strength shot through her, surprising her as much as it did her attacker. Savagely she brought her knee up into his groin, at the same time raking both sets of fingernails across his face, his eyes.

He fell back a step, releasing his grip on her. She lashed out in a high kick, catching him in the chest, then pivoted and ran for the door. As she skimmed down the hallway, she could hear his muttered oaths; her skin prickled at the foulness in his voice.

She found the stairs quickly, elated that her instincts had proven correct. In flight, the odds were with her. The house was familiar to her, and she could dodge furniture and find doorways much more easily than he. If she could only reach the patio doors . . . *Why,* she wondered, *did they seem so far away?* Through the distortion of fear, time crept with an agonizing slowness, and it seemed long minutes rather than mere seconds since the chase began. With each step, she anticipated a touch, a hideous breath in her ear.

At the bottom of the stairs, she swerved abruptly to the left, into the study. The French doors leading onto the patio were directly ahead of her, but first she had to get around the desk, skirt the library table . . .

She was picking herself up off the floor before she even realized she had fallen. A footfall behind her was close, too close. She screamed again as he grabbed her hair, twisting it around his hand to pull her back against him.

His breath whispered across her cheek, deceptively gentle. His words—*what was he saying?* she couldn't tell, didn't want to know—*felt* slimy and putrid. If she had ever before considered stark terror, she would have never imagined it to be so *total*, wrapping around every nerve until there was nothing left of oneself.

Then the words were no longer in her ear. They were in her mind, not only the words, but feelings—fear, rage, sickening lust, perverted pleasure in the pain he was creating. As her mind, her other sense, responded to the signals, her familiar view of the world receded into an indistinct blur, replaced by carnival fun-house images, all twisted, distorted, magnified into terrifying proportions. Everything was threatening, dangerous; no one understood, everyone was a potential enemy, and he/she had to make them pay for what they had done. They would all die horribly, with blood running thick red; it felt so *good* to twist the knife . . .

She screamed, the sound tearing up through her throat, and she twisted away in one desperate, savage burst of strength, so that the knife blade only slid halfway round her neck.

Her flesh stung and burned, but she barely noticed it, so intent was she on clawing her way out of that morass of otherworldly ugliness. She didn't even notice the sudden light that blazed in the room, the commotion of bodies and voices rushing in, shouting, running.

"How the hell did he get through?"

"Grab him!"

"God, she's . . . !"

"Watch it! Get the knife!"

She was content to sink onto the floor and lay quietly; she was so very tired—and so *cold*. Lost was a very painful place to be.

A tall blue figure stood over her. He wavered in the light like a mirage, and his voice was strangely fuzzy. "You'd better call an ambulance. He cut her throat."

Chapter One

WINTER WAS LATE this year and the last few days of autumn sparkled over the countryside with a bright warmth that belied the forecast of freezing temperatures within the next forty-eight hours. Aspen and cottonwood glowed bright yellow and gold in the sunlight in a last flashy display before frost would leave the trees bare and skeletal against the sky.

Sloane stood for a moment beside her car, looking around the little town with deep pleasure. Not much more than a hamlet, it nestled in the Rockies with serene indifference to its size. Neat frame houses, many in the distinctive turreted style of the early 1900s, lined the short main street up to the town square. Small quaint shops, which supported the town during the tourist season, hugged the square on all sides. Around and among nearly all the buildings, trees and shrubs grew in profusion, creating a subtle blend of nature and civilization that Sloane found utterly charming. She never tired of the scenery or the weather or the peaceful solitude. She was glad she had come.

Her eyes came to rest on the shop directly in front of her, calling her attention back to the reason for being in town today. This was Johanssen's Gift Shop, more a miniature art gallery than a boutique, where local artists and craftsmen could display their handiwork on a consignment basis. During the season, Sloane came by weekly to bring in new pieces of sculpture and to see which of the others had sold.

She hadn't planned to bring anything else in until the spring, until Carol's call the night before. Paul van Buren, owner of the most prestigious gallery in Denver, was going to be at Johanssen's today on one of his periodic ''discovery'' trips, and Carol, as his senior assistant, thought it would be an ideal time for Sloane to bring her talent to his attention. Sloane readily agreed.

As Sloane's car was the only one in the immediate vicinity of the gift shop, Carol and van Buren apparently hadn't yet arrived. That was all right with her; she hadn't planned to meet the great man in person, much preferring to drop off the new pieces along with a short note to Carol, pick up her mail, and be on her way.

Margaret Johanssen, a plump, smiling little woman, greeted Sloane at the door.

"My goodness, I didn't expect to see you again for a while, Sloane. But then I guess Carol told you about Mr. van Buren," she said with a speculative glance at the small box Sloane held so carefully.

"Yes, she called last night. I've brought two new things. Tell me what you think." Gently she set the box on a small table near the door and lifted two statuettes from the shredded newspaper where they were safely nestled.

Both figures were small but exquisitely shaped. The larger one was a burro with a full pack, frozen in the act of rubbing his rump blissfully against a rough fence post. The other was a delicate miniature owl with nestlings, one wing drawn protectively across her wide-eyed face.

"Oh, these are wonderful," breathed Margaret, "the best you've done; van Buren will love them." Her round face beamed enchantment.

"I hope you're right." Sloane, too, was pleased with her latest work and couldn't quite keep the pride out of her voice. "From what I've heard, he doesn't impress easily. But who knows, I just might get lucky." She handed Margaret a neatly folded sheet of paper. "Here's a note for Carol. Will you give it to her and ask her to call me tonight?"

"But aren't you going to stay?" asked Margaret in surprise. "They should be here soon."

"Oh, no," Sloane protested, laughing. "When I meet Paul van Buren, I don't want to look like Annie Oakley." She slid her hands down her sides, brushing at the red plaid shirt and snug, faded jeans that were her standard wardrobe except for special occasions. "Besides, I'd rather not be here looking on while he pronounces judgment."

"With a figure like yours, I doubt he'd pay much attention to how you're dressed. But I do see your point about not being here. It would be like waiting for the teacher to grade your final exam and then announce it to the whole class." She patted Sloane's hand affectionately. "I'll see Carol gets your note. Call and let me know if you become an overnight celebrity. I want some credit for being your very first patron!"

Smiling and waving, Sloane left Johanssen's and angled across the square to the tiny post office, enjoying the soft warmth of the sun against her face. Like most of the other buildings in Snowcrest, the post office was unpretentious and homey, its tan clapboards scrupulously neat and free from any chipped or peeling paint. As usual for that time of day, there were few customers, but the two women who passed Sloane on their way out smiled pleasantly. She didn't know their names, but she enjoyed the friendliness as she enjoyed almost everything about the little town.

She opened the box and removed the mail, noticing idly that there was more volume than usual. *Probably more bills,* she thought, shuffling through the letters. The electric bill and MasterCard statement were right on time; then one piece in particular arrested her attention, and she looked at it closely.

The envelope seemed harmless enough, a white rectangle, standard business size, neatly typed with her address: "Sloane Taylor, P.O. Box 913, Snowcrest, Colorado." But the return address with her ex-husband's name was a bit startling. It had been well over two years since she'd last heard from him, and certainly she'd never expected to be in touch with him again. Their parting had been anything but friendly; even after all this time, she was uncomfortable with any thoughts of that period—first the estrangement, then Rena's death and her own . . . injury. More had happened in those few months than in all her previous twenty-eight years.

Well, maybe Michael had found a hidden portfolio of stocks that required her signature. If it had to do with money, Michael would write a letter to the Devil and probably expect an immediate reply.

As she began to rip off the end of the envelope, a queer prickle of apprehension teased at her mind. It was a too-familiar sensation, one she'd not felt in three years, since that night . . . *No,* she commanded herself. *No more flashes. I don't want that anymore!* But the feeling persisted and grew stronger. A sudden chill, like an icy blast of wind rising from nowhere, shook her body, raising the fine hairs on her forearms.

Unconsciously, her hand crept up to her neck to cover the long, thin scar that extended in a semi-circle from under her jaw more than halfway around her throat. She knew, without reading the words, that it had to do with *him*.

Her eyes scanned the page quickly, searching. And she found it in the second paragraph: *Chapman*. An image of his face leapt into her memory. Even worse, the recollection of her own mind being sucked into the cesspool of his private, insane limbo . . . The message was unmistakable. She wasn't yet free of Chapman; it wasn't over; maybe it would never be over. The knowledge left her shaken with nausea.

He watched her from across the room, wondering at her unnatural stillness as she clutched the letter in one trembling hand. Her skin was ashen against a cloud of long, dark hair and seemed to be drawn tightly across high cheekbones; her wide-set brown eyes appeared to be vacant and staring, but he recognized the expression as fear and knew her gaze was turned inward on dark, secret thoughts that could not be shared. He was unnerved by the surge of attraction and concern he felt just from looking at her.

Those frightened doe-eyes reminded him of someone, but the memory eluded him. No matter. He would remember in time. Right now, it suddenly seemed vital that he break her painful concentration and bring her lovely face back to life.

Holding his mail as though glancing through it, he strode briskly forward, his boot heels clicking against the floor tiles. His elbow bumped abruptly against her arm and she gasped, whirling around, one hand still pressed against her throat.

He grasped her arm, steadying her. "Didn't mean to knock you down. Are you all right?" His voice was deep and calming, and she looked up at him gratefully.

"Yes—yes, I'm fine. I should apologize to you. I was standing right in your way—right in everyone's way, I'm afraid," she added, glancing around as though she had just become aware of her surroundings.

"My pleasure. It saved me the trouble of finding an excuse to meet you."

Startled, she looked back at him. Tall as she was, he was at least half a foot taller, towering over her. His gray eyes were warm and humorous and startlingly light against the deep tan of his skin and the blackness of his hair. He was rugged-looking, and his clothing lent credence to her mental picture of him astride a horse, surrounded by livestock and free spaces. He looked every inch a rancher in his jeans, boots, and denim jacket—his thick, straight hair only partially covered by a brown Stetson.

He was easily the most attractive man she'd ever seen, and she was alarmed at her response to him—or maybe appalled was a better term. Hadn't she decided to keep all her relationships on a casual footing? And there was nothing casual about her pulse rate. *Be careful, Sloane,* her guardian voice chided.

"Wish I knew what was going on behind those brown eyes," he drawled. "Looks like a mighty interesting conversation."

She smiled somewhat stiffly, annoyed with herself for staring and disconcerted by his swift perception. "I was just trying to decide if I like the direct approach." *God, am I flirting?*

"And . . . ?"

What the hell, she thought, reaching her decision swiftly before prudence got the better of her. She was tired of being careful. "And I think I do. At least I won't have to worry about being bored."

He laughed, a totally male, very pleasing sound. "I think we're going to have a lot in common. Can I buy you a cup of coffee and tantalize you with my wit?"

Funny, she thought, *how his smile seemed to radiate, yet his lips barely moved. It's his eyes; are those little crow's feet from squinting against the sun or are they laugh lines?* It really didn't matter. Either way, the effect was devastating.

"Coffee is exactly what I had in mind. How did you know?"

As she preceded him through the door, his eyes followed her slim jean-clad figure. It had been a long time since any woman intrigued him as quickly and as deeply as this one. She was attractive, intelligent, witty, sensual, but so were a lot of other women. There was something else about her, an air of mystery, an aura of fear and distress that roused his protective instincts. And still something niggled at the back of his mind: where had he seen her before?

She tapped her fingernail against the rim of her coffee cup as she gazed absently out the window of the diner at the majestic Rocky Mountains. Blue and gray shadows cast by the October sun chased across crags and crevices, down into valleys overflowing with spruce and aspen, and up again to white-tipped peaks outlined against the sky—all creating a subtly soothing kaleidoscope of shapes and moods. Caught between the visual stimulation of her surroundings and the tension unleashed by the hateful letter in her shoulder bag, she was for a moment annoyed by the intrusion of her companion's voice.

She wrenched both her gaze and her attention back to the man sitting across the table.

He raised one eyebrow slightly in mock reproof. "It seems you *do* bore easily. I've entertained heads of state with that story, but it didn't even rate a smile from you."

A faint flush of embarrassment spread across her cheeks and throat, and he noted it with amusement; he couldn't remember the last time he'd seen a woman blush.

"I'm really sorry," she apologized. "Normally I function a little more gracefully than this."

"Well, bad news affects most of us that way," he commented.

"What?" *Was the man a mind-reader?*

"It was pretty obvious," he explained. "In the post office, I mean. You looked as though you'd had a shock of some kind. Do you want to talk about it?"

His concern touched her. Suddenly she wished she could confide in him, lay it all on his shoulders and say, "Here, it's too heavy to carry alone." But that wasn't her way. Besides, it was all too fantastic for him to believe. Sometimes she didn't believe it herself.

So she answered truthfully, if evasively, "No, it's okay. Just a letter from my ex-husband I'd rather not have to read. Do you realize I don't even know your name?"

He laughed aloud, throwing his head back slightly in a quick motion that immediately endeared him to her. She had a sharp, fierce longing to touch his hair, to see if it felt as crisp and vital as it looked.

"Very neat dodge. You'd make a great diplomat, Miss— See, I don't know your name either, but I wasn't going to make an issue of it."

"Point for you," she grinned. Amazingly, she was enjoying this encounter more than she would have thought possible. The worry about Chapman and the hateful letter tucked away in her bag began slipping into the background. "I'm Sloane Taylor. And you?"

He shook his head. "First woman I ever met who didn't want to talk about herself. Where'd you come from? Not from around here, I know, or I'd have run into you long before now." His gaze was intent, and he saw her tension return and her grip tighten on the coffee cup.

"I'm from Dallas originally. About three years ago I moved to Denver, then I found a place in the mountains, not far from Snowcrest."

"And what do you do in the mountains, not far from Snowcrest?"

She couldn't tell if he was just making polite conversation or if his interest in her was genuine. The latter, she suspected. There had been an immediate electricity between them, much too strong to be one-sided. She felt the same, wanting to know anything and everything about him, but that would be a dangerous game to play. Intimacy was too easily fostered when people spoke of their pasts; for now, she preferred to keep it light.

"Well," she answered finally, "I look at the scenery a lot. There's a lot of it around here, you know."

"If you expect me to believe you're nothing more than a wealthy, bored socialite who decided to take the alimony and head for the hills, you're out of luck." He gestured toward her hands in answer to her unspoken question. "For one thing, your fingernails aren't long enough."

Her eyes followed his gaze and unwillingly she saw what he meant, what many men wouldn't have noticed. Her hands were soft and well tended but apparently strong; her nails were clean of polish, shiny from buffing but very short; even her wrists, though slender, were far from fragile.

"Another point for you," she conceded. "I'm a sculptor. I have a studio in the cabin, and I get most of my supplies from Denver, so I don't come in to Snowcrest very often."

"And my foreman usually drives in for our supplies, but he's down with a sprained knee, so the duty fell to me. Guess luck was on my side today." To cover the awkward silence that followed, he added, "Now that we've solved the mystery of not having met sooner, tell me more about your work. And why you left Dallas. Surely a city that size could support a struggling artist."

"Oh, no. It's your turn now. I still don't know your name."

He leaned back comfortably against his chair. "If we're taking turns, we must be playing a game," he teased. "You can have the name—Lucas Santee—but the rest I leave to your imagination. Ten points for every right answer."

"That might not be the smartest thing you've ever done, Santee. My imagination is a force to be reckoned with." She paused, uncomfortably aware of the truth that lay behind the easy banter. She prayed he'd never find out just how forceful her imagination could be.

"Prove it." He extended his right hand, palm

up. "My secrets are all here before you, waiting to be revealed."

"You asked for it." Taking his hand in her own, she raised his palm closer, tracing his lifeline with the forefinger of her free hand. "I see a proud, independent man of great strength," she intoned in a bad imitation of Bela Lugosi. "He is tall and dark . . ." A tingle, not unlike a mild electric current, nipped at her hand, ran up her arm, her neck, into her head. Sudden visions, clear yet confusing and frightening, intruded into her own mental space, and instinctively she pushed back at them. *Not again. Leave me alone!*

"What's wrong?"

He was quick, this man. He saw too much, too clearly. *Think fast.* "I'm just out of practice. It took a second or two to fall back and regroup." She fell back into character, deciding to tell the small, obvious truths that would arouse no suspicion. "You have powerful emanations, Dark Stranger." *Charismatic.* "You are a born leader of men, and wealth is within your grasp." *Successful, respected, responsible.* "You are a man of character and vision, tempered with the merciful qualities of tenderness and compassion." *Conscientious, caring, responsive—a special man.*

He grinned disarmingly. "Is that silly accent part of the curriculum at Fortune-Telling Tech?"

"Yep. Lesson One. It wasn't my best class."

"Well, get on with it. Do you foresee any immediate improvements in my boring love life?"

20

She shook her head firmly. "Sorry. You've cast aspersions on my craft, and the spell is broken. You'll just have to find out for yourself."

"I can wait." His voice was quiet, his tone mild, but it held a wealth of meaning. She had to look away from the desire she saw reflected in his eyes.

She changed the subject abruptly. "How large is your ranch?"

"I didn't tell you I was a rancher."

Stupid, stupid! "Simple deduction, my dear Watson. What else would a man in those clothes do in this part of the state? You didn't tell me one of your parents was Native American, either, but it's literally written all over your face."

He shrugged, seeming to accept her explanation. "My place isn't as large as some around here, but it's big enough to take up most of my time. We run some cattle but mostly saddle horses and rodeo stock."

"Sounds like a full-time operation. You must put in a lot of long, hard hours."

"Sure. But I'm used to it. Dad made sure I learned everything there was to know about ranching when I was just a tadpole, including all the manual labor. He and my mother had the roughest part, building the place ftom scratch. They even started out in the traditional log cabin—built it themselves. It's still standing, and surprisingly, it's in pretty good condition. No, the hardest work was done before I was born. Dad turned that place into a productive ranch. I just inherited it.''

She loved the pride that crept into his voice when he spoke of his parents. For maybe the millionth time, she longed for that kind of memory, a close-knit, loving family, a mother to come home to . . .

''And you've never lived anywhere else?'' she probed, moving away from her uncomfortable thoughts.

''Served a hitch in the service, then I came right back home. By that time my folks were both dead, and I had both the ranch and a little sister to take care of. Besides, I never saw another place I'd rather be.'' He gestured toward the panorama spread before them through the window. ''You must know what I mean. Something brought you here.''

Yes, she thought, *something did. How would he react if I said, ''A girl, now dead, once told me about her home town, how lovely and peaceful it was, so I came here to heal my soul''?*

Their eyes met and held; she stopped breathing while an elemental awareness swept through her being.

''What is it about you, lady?'' he whispered. ''When I look at you I hear music.''

Sloane's pulse leapt, both in response and in sudden alarm. It was moving much too fast—with nowhere to go. She swallowed, feeling suffocated by the surfeit of emotion.

''I—I have to go,'' she stammered, gathering

22

her bag for flight. "I was supposed to be in Denver—to pick up some supplies."

His large brown hand touched her lightly. "I'm sorry. I really don't know why I said that. Believe it or not, flowery phrases aren't my style, especially with women I've just met."

"I know. And it isn't you. It's just . . ." Her words trailed off ineffectually.

He didn't press her to stay but rose from the table with her. As they walked out into the crisp autumn morning together, he placed his hand on her arm. The imprint of his fingers burned through her sleeve.

When she looked into his face, his dark features were guarded, but she felt the tension of awareness flowing between them and knew he was as affected by it as she.

"It's not over, you know," he said softly. "I'll be seeing you, Sloane Taylor." Slate gray eyes locked with brown, and she felt a thrill of anticipation at the promise.

She took the mountain drive slowly, thinking about the morning and its unsettling events. How strange that he had come into her life on this particular day. Was it a prophetic meeting, somehow linking the three of them—Chapman, Santee, and herself? She hoped not, but she had an uneasy premonition that fate was playing a nasty trick. She had been drawn into both their minds, Chapman's and Santee's, and that forged a bond that just might be unbreakable.

* * *

Lucas Santee was a big man in every way. He thought big, dreamed big, and succeeded on a grand scale. When he loved, it was wholeheartedly, and his hatred could be equally passionate. He generally tried to keep his emotions under tight rein, especially in the past few years, and there were few people or situations that elicited an extreme response from him.

But since leaving Sloane Taylor that morning, he hadn't been able to concentrate on anything else. Apart from her beauty, which was undeniable, she was a challenge, a lovely enigma, tantalizingly mysterious for several reasons. First, she was alone and, he suspected, frightened. Then there was her reclusiveness; she must have deliberately hidden herself away or surely he'd have met her before now. Most of all, there was that hint of recognition, the unsettling feeling that he knew her or should know her. And now a new, more disturbing element had been added: it was almost as though he were afraid to remember her, as though the knowledge would be distasteful—or dangerous.

On the desk in his study, where he sat sorting the morning's mail, sat a small gold picture frame holding a snapshot of a pretty young woman with wildly flying golden-brown hair and a pert, sassy face. He remembered so clearly the day he had taken that picture; it was only minutes before she had driven away, off on her own for the very first time. As always, he felt a sharp pang of grief thinking about her. God, he missed her so, her sweetness, their closeness. It was still so hard to accept—dead at twenty, because a crazy man thought she was someone else, someone named Mrs. Michael Fielding.

A frown creased his forehead as he gazed at the photograph of his young sister. Then awareness dawned.

Cursing softly, he opened the bottom desk drawer and withdrew a large manila folder. Sorting swiftly through the contents, he stopped dead when his fingers touched a worn, folded newspaper clipping. A faded wire photo headed the column of newsprint. It wasn't a clear picture, but it was enough. As he looked at it, his eyes grew icy with hatred for Sloane Taylor.

Driving up the winding road that led to the A-frame cabin, Sloane breathed deeply, savoring the pungent forest scents. This was always her favorite time of any day, this homecoming.

The house was well sheltered against both the wind and the idle curious; it came into view unexpectedly around the last curve. With the sunlight glinting off the tall windows, reflecting into the sentinel trees nearby, it was easy to imagine she was entering a fortress, her own private castle where trouble and danger were not allowed to intrude.

As she unlocked the front door, thinking about the letter she must read, she was grateful for the physical security of the cabin. Iron bars and security screens, double locks and deadbolts had been installed by the previous owner who, according to the realtor, had owned a priceless collection of antique weapons and spent a great portion of his time traveling. When Sloane moved in, she had thought the bars an eyesore and would have had them removed but for the expense. Now she blessed them.

Once inside, she decided there was no use procrastinating; she ought to read the letter and be done with it. She arranged herself on and among the pillows in the center of the floor and faced the fireplace; removing the letter from its envelope, she unfolded it and began to read.

> *Dear Sloane,*
>
> *I hesitate to write this letter because I don't wish to cause you undue anxiety over a matter which will, I feel sure, come to nothing. But after serious reflection I have decided it is your right to be apprised of the current situation.*

Oh, Michael, she thought tiredly, *you still sound like a pompous jerk.*

> *Last week Mrs. Evans came to me with a tale of a prowler lurking about the grounds. Blake investigated and reported seeing, although briefly, a man who strongly resembled*

Gerald Chapman. Of course, I immediately contacted the authorities.

Sloane, Chapman has been released. Before you panic, please bear in mind that there is absolutely no proof it was he who trespassed. His doctors are quite convinced he is truly rehabilitated; he was released into his brother's care and is employed at a small construction firm here in Dallas.

At any rate, he knew you as Sloane Fielding, not Taylor, and there is no reason for him to suspect you have moved to Colorado. You've covered your tracks well; even I can't contact you except through the post office, so please try to keep the proper perspective about this.

Although our marriage is over, I still feel a deep responsibility toward you and bitter regret that things ended as they did. The fault lies with me and my blind ambition. Sloane, I would like to talk to you about this as well as other matters. Please send me your telephone number or call me.

I think of you often.

> *Fondly, Michael*

Sloane wasn't sure what she felt, but she thought it was anger. Dear Michael. Michael, with his "authorities" and "proper perspectives" and don't-get-involved-Sloane and you've-put-me-in-an-intolerable-position-Sloane and you-brought-it-on-yourself-

Sloane and I-won't-allow-you-to-jeopardize-my-career-Sloane. Responsibility, regret, fault, Michael? Fondness, Michael? *Go to hell, Michael.*

The little apartment was dark, dank, and smelly. A dim overhead bulb barely lit the corner where the man lay on a small cot, wrapped in a thin blanket against the slight chill of November in Dallas. He fingered a limp, worn newspaper photo with a grimy hand, looking at it intently.

The picture, though indistinct, was clear in his mind—a young woman, attractive, patrician, lovely. He saw through her act, though. From the first day he'd seen her, he had recognized the corruption lurking behind those big brown eyes. Just like the other one.

Everybody had loved *her*, too. Especially the men—troops of them, in and out of her bedroom at night, sneaking down the darkened hallway. "Shhh," she'd whisper, "the brat's asleep. Let's keep it that way." It hadn't taken him long to learn not to mention the midnight visitors; *she* didn't like it. A well-aimed clothes hanger or electric cord taught him early the wisdom of silence.

Oh, sure, she'd put on a good act, he'd give her that. In front of strangers, she cooed and clucked and hugged him. "My sweet little man," she'd croon, "Mama just couldn't do without her baby." She always smelled so good.

They were all the same, really. They smiled and batted their eyelashes and smelled of sweet perfume and said pretty words. But they lied. They all lied.

Especially this one. Miss Do-Gooder. Lady Bountiful. But she had proven to be like all the rest, enticing him, then rejecting him, ultimately trying to destroy him.

In one respect, though, she was different—she was smart. Twice before he'd tried to make her pay; each time she'd escaped his justice. But not this time. He'd had three long years to think about it. This time she wouldn't get away.

It won't be long now, Mrs. Fielding. Will you be glad to see me?

Chapter Two

SHE WAS AWARE that she was dreaming, but the knowledge brought no comfort. If anything, it only added to her terror, because no matter how hard she willed it, she couldn't wake up. For a split second she feared she would be eternally trapped in this other plane, forever seeking escape from the horror that pursued her.

Then the dream itself took over, and once more she was caught up in the fantasy that blended her past with her fears of the future.

In the surrealistic way of dreams, she was running through a dense white fog that swirled and eddied into ominously spectral shapes, yet she wasn't really going anywhere. She seemed to be on a treadmill, while behind her the Hunter effortlessly gained on her with each passing second.

Her legs burned with fatigue, but she wasn't permitted to rest; fear controlled her body and she had to obey, so she blindly fled the crawling, insidious terror pursuing her. She was afraid to look back and afraid not to, for what would be worse: to see him and know he was there, or not to see him and never be sure where he was? Her heart felt as though it would burst with the burden of her flight; her throat ached from the rasping breaths that never quite brought enough air into her starved lungs. Soon now, she knew, her tortured body would collapse.

But there, suddenly, ahead of her through the mist, she could see a figure silhouetted in a doorway. Though his face was in darkness, she knew him, and she called to him for help. "Michael, I'm here, over here! Please, I need you!" But her voice wouldn't carry through the dense air; she watched her words, iridescent in the fog, falter and drift to the ground, bouncing as they landed.

The shadow man stepped back through the open door into a brightly lit room. For just a second, she could see him clearly as he carefully straightened his tie. Then he closed the door. "No! Michael, let me in!" She pounded on the door, putting every ounce of strength she possessed into the effort; but always, just at the moment of contact, time slowed, dragging heavily against her arms so the blows never landed.

She turned her back to the door and leaned against it, looking straight ahead to her fate. The

Hunter loomed out of the fog, smiling and slowly shaking his head. "Didn't you know you couldn't escape? You got away from me twice before, but no more, no more." He crooned the words in a hypnotic drone that sapped the rest of her strength and will as she watched him take the knife from his pocket and click the blade out with a press of his thumb.

Her senses became suddenly more acute as her body weakened. She could feel the cold, damp mist chilling her skin and hear the sound of her heart thudding wildly against her ribs; his odor was pungent and sharp in her nostrils, and the taste of fear rose in her throat, acrid and bitter as bile. The knife moved closer to her face, held now by a disembodied hand. On the cutting edge she could see a dark stain gleaming wetly, and she knew the blood was Rena's—knew, too, the scream rising in her throat would never be uttered. After all, who was there to hear? But she heard it in her head, the scream, high and sharp and rising, and it went on and on and became the sound of a siren, shrill and piercing, but she knew it would be too late . . .

Her eyes snapped open to darkness, the echoes of her scream fading away. The dream was over but, as always, it lingered in her dry throat and painfully clenched fists. After several long minutes, her heartbeat slowed, her stomach stopped heaving, her breath evened out.

Trembling legs supported her as far as the bathroom. She flipped the light switch next to the lavatory mirror, shutting her eyes momentarily to the startling reflection. With trembling fingers she touched the darkened skin under her eyes, wiping away the useless tears. *Did Rena Davidson look like this as she died,* Sloane wondered; *was she wide-eyed and pale with terror? Did her mouth and throat go dry so that she couldn't scream for help?*

Sloane was unutterably weary. She just couldn't face the rest of the night wondering if she would see Chapman's obscene face every time she closed her eyes. From the medicine cabinet she took a prescription bottle and shook out a tiny triangular yellow pill. It had been nearly a year since she last needed to take one, but now she was glad she hadn't thrown them away. For tonight, at least, there would be no more dreams.

Morning was too early and too bright. The sun burst through the double glass doors of the combination loft/bedroom/studio onto her face. With a groan she pulled a pillow over her head. Tuesday was nothing special, she reasoned groggily, so why bother to get up? She could spend the day in bed nursing this damned headache.

Headache? Was she coming down with something? She had felt fine yesterday . . . Then it all jolted into place—Michael's letter, the dream, the little yellow pill.

Close by, the telephone shrilled commandingly. It was several moments before her nerveless hand found the receiver. "Yes?" Her voice was no more than a dry croak, so she tried again. "Yes, hello?"

"Sloane? Were you still asleep? Lord, it's nearly ten o'clock! And I thought you were the original early bird."

"I was just getting up, Carol. I don't feel too well this morning."

"You sound strange. I hope you're not coming down with that darned flu. Two of our people have been out with it for nearly a week." Typically, Carol sailed into the next topic without waiting to find out if Sloane had the flu or bubonic plague. "Listen, darling, I'm sorry I didn't call you last night, but I met the most heavenly man! Can you meet me for lunch tomorrow? One o'clock at the Watering Hole, okay?" In the background, Sloane could hear another voice murmuring, claiming Carol's attention.

"I don't know, Carol, maybe another day . . ." she began.

"That's fine, darling. Don't be late; I'll be on a tight schedule. Gotta run. See you tomorrow."

Carol's selective deafness certainly took all the argument out of a conversation, Sloane thought wryly, replacing the receiver. She didn't have anything else planned for tomorrow though, and she always enjoyed seeing Carol. But she wasn't quite sure why her friend had called in the first place. Something about not having time to call last night. Of course, the note she had left for Carol with

Margaret Johanssen, asking her to call with van Buren's verdict. Apparently she wouldn't find out until tomorrow.

As she lay staring at the ceiling, effectively wakened by Carol's call, all the disturbing events of the previous day came creeping back, though she wasn't at all sure she was prepared to face them. Michael's letter. She still couldn't quite believe it. The single typed page still lay, folded, on the nightstand. It menaced her quietly, like a snake coiled and waiting to strike.

She reread it slowly. It was dated nearly a week before. Maybe by now Michael would have some news.

Michael answered on the third ring. Sloane was mildly surprised by the lack of emotion she felt at hearing his voice: no pangs, no twinges, no instant replay of the last painful scene. He was merely a pleasant voice at the end of a telephone wire.

"Michael Fielding."

"Hello, Michael. It's Sloane."

"Sloane! It's good to hear from you. How are you?"

Did she only imagine the rush of warmth in his tone? Did he truly think of her with fondness? "I'm fine, thank you. I decided it would be best if you had my number, just in case. Do you have something to write on?"

"Yes, I'm right here at the desk. Go ahead."

She could picture him in the study by the antique oak desk that was one of his prized possessions, looking every inch the well-groomed young professional in gray flannel. Appearances were very important to Michael.

She gave him the number, hoping she could keep the conversation brief without being rude. A long discussion with her ex-husband wasn't high on her list of priorities.

"Sloane, about Chapman . . ."

"It's all right, Michael. I haven't let it throw me. But I do want to know everything you find out."

"I've hired a man to do some checking for me. Chapman's working with a construction firm in north Dallas and has kept all his outpatient appointments with the mental health clinic. So far, he's been a model citizen, but if he makes one wrong move, I'll know." He was silent for a moment and Sloane tensed, knowing what was coming. "I should have been there for you then, Sloane, that night. What I did was unforgivable . . ."

"Don't, Michael. It's over. We're over." She blinked back threatening tears. What it must have cost him to say that! "We've both grown since then, but not together. We were never really together, you know that."

"I suppose it's pointless to ask you to come back."

"Yes."

His sigh came faintly across the line. "Take care of yourself, darling. If you need me . . ."

"I'll remember. Thank you, Michael."

As she dropped the receiver into its cradle, she

wanted to curse, throw something, punch his face in. *Why now, Michael, when it's too late? Three years too late.* If she were honest with herself, she would say eight years too late. The gift of hindsight was wonderfully revealing. It enabled her to see clearly, for the very first time, that her relationship with Michael had been doomed from the start, for too many reasons. He had been looking for a hostess, the "right kind of wife," someone who would enhance his image. And what had she been looking for? Security, acceptance, a place to belong, all the things she'd lacked as a child. Not exactly the best reasons for undertaking so serious a step as marriage.

But even so, it might have worked—*might* have, except for her "peculiarity." It had haunted her, frightened her, all her life. She could remember, all too vividly, the crawling horror she'd felt the first time she had consciously "read" someone, had realized she was actually tuned in to another mind. It became her secret, zealously guarded so no one else would know she was a freak.

Not surprisingly, it had appalled Michael. Maybe if she'd told him in the beginning, he wouldn't have been so shocked the first time she read him. On the other hand, if he hadn't had so much to hide, it wouldn't have mattered so much. As it was, she had learned not to mention her flashes; and as long as she remained silent about the things she picked up, Michael was prepared to ignore her psi abilities.

Their mutual silence was an added strain for her. She could never talk to Michael about the burden she carried, her nightmarish childhood, the foster homes. . . . That part of her life she didn't really want to discuss, only to forget. Sometimes, though, she couldn't help but wish for a caring, sensitive friend to confide in. There had only been a few others in her life who understood and cared, the friends she had made at the psychic research center where she had gone to test her abilities and to learn to control them to a certain extent. Then she'd met Michael and, in deference to his wishes, had weaned herself away from what he'd termed "an unhealthy dependence on a cult of oddballs."

Thank God they'd never wanted to start a family. Sloane had long ago decided she would never have children, would never pass along this curse. It was one of the few things in which she and Michael had been in complete agreement. Looking back, she couldn't find anything else she and Michael had shared. Once she had asked him, shortly before their wedding, why he wanted to marry her, a social nonentity, when he could have made a much more "proper" alliance with someone of his own class.

"Because of your determination, darling," he'd replied, kissing the tip of her nose. "Even with all the strikes against you, you rose above your upbringing, put yourself through college, educated yourself in all the social graces. Why, just looking at you, no one would guess your background." He had grinned disarmingly. "With your drive and my ambition, I'll be the youngest president in history."

Young, in love, and with more security than she'd ever known, Sloane refused to see the pomposity, the snobbery, behind his remarks. She was determined to live up to his image of her, never dreaming that he had never really seen her at all, only what he wanted to be there.

Even later, when the marriage was obviously failed, he would, from time to time, fall back into the fantasy. "Sloane, I just don't understand you. What has love got to do with this? You're wealthy, you're comfortable, and a divorce would serve no purpose that I can see. Really, I sometimes feel I'm talking to a complete stranger." With both their futures at stake, they remained poles apart.

No, their marriage had never had a fair chance. It could best be described as an uneasy truce, one which had flared into open hostilities about six months before the divorce. Against her better judgment, she had agreed not to file until his campaign was over and the election decided. If she wouldn't listen to reason, Michael argued, she could at least support him until then. He was so confident of victory that he had never once considered that he might lose. And when he was in office, he told her, he could weather the scandal of a divorce and continue to build his career.

She had told Michael the truth. It was over. She wanted it to be over. She would never again trust him; an intimate relationship would be impossible now. In fact, she had doubts that she would ever again be willing to become that close to anyone. Intimacy, for her, would always be painful.

Yet there was Santee. That immediate, electrifying attraction. Would she be willing to risk it for him? Would she even be given the choice? She thought not. All she could do was wait. And hope.

The drive into Snowcrest only took about fifteen minutes and included several breathtaking views. Sloane never had her fill of the Rockies and usually looked forward to the drive. Today, though, she would rather have stayed at home; she had a lot more thinking to do, and she wasn't feeling her best. Last night her sleep had been plagued with the dreams again, and she was mentally exhausted. Another pill had provided much-needed rest, but did nothing to combat the depression closing in on her.

It was nearly one-fifteen when she arrived at the restaurant, and Carol was visibly impatient.

"Good Lord, Sloane, where have you been? You know what a fuss the old man makes if I'm late back from lunch. And today, of all days!" Carol, despite her veneer of cool blonde sophistication, could occasionally fly into a snit that her friends tried to overlook whenever possible. "I *told* you I wouldn't have much time! Really, it's not like you to be so inconsiderate."

"Sorry, it couldn't be helped," Sloane returned

mildly. She'd learned that Carol's tantrums passed more quickly when they were ignored. "What's so special about today?"

Carol was clearly bursting with news and could barely contain herself. She clasped her perfectly manicured hands together in a theatrical gesture that would have looked ridiculous on anyone else.

"Sloane, he loved your work! He bought everything of yours that Margaret had on display, and he wants to see you to discuss, among other things, an exhibit! Can you believe it?" Carol's heavily mascaraed blue eyes danced with excitement as she leaned forward to watch Sloane's reaction.

Incredibly, Sloane had forgotten about Mr. van Buren, her career, everything, in the emotional storm of the past couple of days. She looked at her friend blankly.

"What is the matter with you, Sloane? You aren't even *listening* to me!" Carol looked so crestfallen that Sloane felt sorry for her.

"Yes, I am. And I'm thrilled. Just bear with me, okay? I had to take a sleeping pill last night, and it hasn't quite worn off yet."

Carol sighed in exasperation. "All right, we'll take it slow. Watch these lips, dear. You—are—a—success. He—wants—to—see—you."

Sloane had to laugh. "I get the message. When?"

"When what?"

"When does he want to see me?"

"As soon as possible, but I'll have to check his schedule."

"Never mind! You work it out and call me. Now what did he say about an exhibit?"

As Carol launched into a blow-by-blow description of her entire conversation with van Buren, Sloane let the words flow over and around her. If Carol looked as self-satisfied as a fairy godmother who had just changed a washcloth into a gold lamé evening gown, Sloane definitely felt like a role model for a modern Cinderella. Sculpture had only been a hobby with her until recently, when she had thrown herself into it obsessively in an effort to heal the wounds inflicted by her recent terrors. As her talent had developed, so had her confidence, but to be singled out in this way was totally unexpected and gratifying.

". . . then he said I should arrange an appointment with you, so here we are. Exciting, isn't it? A star is born!"

"*Unreal* is more like it. I can hardly believe this! Are you sure he was talking about me? Sloane the Unknown?"

Carol's short laugh matched her personality: sharp, brittle, but totally sincere. "Darling, relax and enjoy it, as they say. It's inevitable. Van Buren has a knack for picking winners. And I told you long ago you had a future in the art world. You should learn to respect my opinion."

"Consider yourself respected. I'll never doubt you again."

Just then the waiter presented them with two large shrimp salads. At Sloane's quizzical look,

Carol explained, "When I saw you were going to be late, I decided to go ahead and order. After all, this is what you always have, though I don't know why. You could eat gravy by the gallon and not gain an ounce." Just for a moment, a flicker of envy replaced the warmth in Carol's eyes, a lightning flash that Sloane didn't miss.

"You could say the same about yourself. In fact, you wear one size smaller than I do." Sloane's praise was more than just a sop for Carol's fragile ego; she sincerely thought her friend one of the most attractive women she'd ever known. What a shame, she thought, that a few extra years should make such inroads on Carol's self-image. Not that any of it ever showed. She wore her air of insouciance like a shield. "And you certainly don't lack for male attention. Sometimes I think you only use your apartment as a stopover for changing clothes."

As quickly as the bug of envious discontent had bitten, it disappeared, leaving Carol once again the concerned friend Sloane had grown to love. "And that's just as it should be," Carol returned. "I'd rather wear out than rust out. And I haven't given up trying to convert you to my philosophy. Really, Sloane, you could have half the men in Colorado beating a path to your door and the other half wishing the line weren't so long. Yet you insist on burying yourself among those horrid evergreens. It's just not natural! Whoever are you saving it for?"

Sloane had long since passed beyond the point of being embarrassed or shocked by Carol's frequently risqué and suggestive remarks. For all her blasé worldliness, Carol still harbored secret romantic dreams of being swept off her feet by an adoring Adonis who would cherish her forever, and she had difficulty understanding how any woman could be as unconcerned with romance as Sloane appeared to be.

"Now what would I do with half the men in Colorado? Use them as models?"

"For a start, until your pea brain could come up with a more stimulating idea." Carol flashed a look past Sloane's shoulder and her expression changed subtly, becoming softer and warmer. "Speaking of stimulating ideas, I could come up with a few where he's concerned."

Sloane turned in her chair to follow Carol's gaze. Lucas Santee, imposing and darkly attractive in a gray western-cut suit, stood talking with a group of several men who had apparently just entered the restaurant and were now waiting for a table. She quickly jerked her head around, unwilling for him to catch her gawking. Carol, of course, showed no such reluctance.

"Isn't he fabulous? Not only the best-looking man in the country but rich and eligible too. I wonder what he's doing here? It's been at least a year since I've seen him out and about."

"Do you know him well?" Sloane couldn't help asking.

"Yes, for all the good that does," Carol replied peevishly. "He lives here, you know. I'm surprised you've never met him."

"I may have seen him around somewhere," Sloane replied noncommittally. "If he's not from the city, then how do you know him?"

"You forget, I'm from Snowcrest too. But I chose to escape at the very first opportunity. It was sheer luck you and I met the first time at Johanssen's. I'd just dropped in to say hello to Margaret."

"Do you keep in touch with any other old friends?" Sloane felt like the lowest kind of sneak, pumping Carol for information, but it was an impulse she couldn't resist.

"Others? Oh, you mean besides Lucas. No, not really. Occasionally I run into a couple of people I went to school with when I visit my sister, but most of our high school crowd scattered after graduation. There isn't much of a future in Snowcrest, except for Lucas, of course." It didn't take more than an expression of interest on Sloane's part to keep Carol talking. "His future was ready-made. His father left him the ranch, and it was already a financial success. Lucas has made it even more so. He's a good businessman."

"Were you a serious item in high school, you and Lucas?"

Carol narrowed her eyes speculatively. "I've never known you to be this curious about anyone. Don't tell me you've been smitten?"

Sloane had the grace to blush. "Just small talk. Would you like to change the subject?"

Carol grinned suddenly, an impish smile that made Sloane distinctly uncomfortable. "As a matter of fact, I think the subject is perfect. Far be it from me to discourage the first display of interest you've ever shown in the opposite sex. No, we weren't a 'serious item.' We dated a few times, but it was all just good fun. *I* wouldn't have minded, but Lucas was always a responsible sort, even at eighteen. He knew he was too young to get involved, and then the next year, his folks died, leaving him with the ranch and a baby sister to raise. Somewhere, he found time to do his duty in Vietnam, but I believe he came straight to Snowcrest after his discharge, and here he's stayed. Anyway, he just seemed to have no time for women, other than an occasional date. We've been out to dinner a few times, years ago, but it was nothing special."

Sloane was still embarrassed and furious with herself for having displayed her interest in Santee, especially to Carol, who would have no compunction about trying to play matchmaker. "Really, Carol, there's no need to go on about it. It was just an idle question."

"Idle, my foot!" Carol laughed. "You want to know about my relationship, or lack thereof, with Lucas. I don't blame you, he's dynamite. But not for me, darling."

"Why not for you," Sloane retorted, "if he's such 'dynamite'?"

"Well, granted, he's a doll. But we never really clicked, you know? Lucas is the original homebody and so blasted *serious*. There was just no common ground, other than having gone to school together. So, sweetie, you have a clear field, with no other competition in sight."

Sloane was trying to frame a suitable reply to close the subject, but she needn't have bothered. Carol had her teeth into it and wasn't about to let go.

"In fact, you might be just what Lucas needs right now. Since Rena's death he rarely leaves the ranch, from what my sister says. He absolutely adored that child. She was like his very own. She was only five when the parents died, so naturally she and Lucas were very close."

The name caught Sloane's attention; only the night before she'd been thinking of another girl named Rena who had also died. "There was quite an age difference between them?" she probed, dreading what was coming, but desperately needing to know.

"Well, she was his half-sister," Carol explained. "His father died when Lucas was quite young, about ten or so, maybe twelve. Anyway, his mother married the ranch foreman a few years later, Art Davidson, and Rena was their child."

Sloane was suddenly very, very cold. "What happened to her—to Rena?" If her voice sounded as stifled as she felt, Carol seemed not to notice.

"That was the really tragic thing. She was murdered, Sloane. From what I've heard, some lunatic escaped from an institution and went after some politician's wife. He mistook Rena for the other woman and cut her throat. That's all secondhand, of course. It happened in Dallas, as a matter of fact. You probably read about it. Anyway, Lucas isn't quite over it. Rena was his only family and a pretty special person. Everyone in Snowcrest loved her.''

Numbed, Sloane couldn't respond. Her mind whirled, rebelling against all she'd just heard. She remembered Rena mentioning her brother. In fact, she'd checked the local phone book once, out of curiosity, but she'd been looking for Davidson, not Santee.

Then a voice behind her penetrated her thoughts.

''. . . seen you for a while, Carol. How have you been?''

''Terrific, as usual, Lucas. I was surprised to see you in here. It's been so long.''

''The Cattlemen's Association wanted a new place to hold our luncheon meetings, so we decided to try the Watering Hole this month.''

''Well, while you're here, I'd like you to meet a friend of mine, Sloane Taylor.''

Turning so that her face was fully revealed to him, Sloane looked up and smiled, praying she could successfully hide the shock she was feeling. ''Hello, Santee.''

All expression disappeared from his face as though a shutter had been slammed on a warmly lit room. "Miss Taylor and I have met, Carol," he stated coldly, his eyes as chilling as his tone. "I'd like to stay and talk, but I have to chair the meeting."

He walked abruptly away, leaving Carol with her mouth agape in astonishment and Sloane with a cold lump somewhere in the region of her heart. Was that really the same man she'd met only two days before? The warm and laughing man with sparkling eyes?

Carol's voice called her from that sense of bewilderment. "I suppose I'd be wasting my time to ask what that was all about."

" 'Fraid so. I honestly don't have a clue." But she did have at least the glimmer of one. Rena's death. He must have connected her with what had happened to his sister. Nothing else could explain his behavior. "Maybe I just rub him the wrong way."

Carol's left eyebrow raised in a quizzical arch. "Now why aren't I surprised you said that?" She shrugged expressively and took a bite of salad. "That's okay," she mumbled around the lettuce, "I'll find out sooner or later."

"Yes," Sloane sighed, "you probably will. And when you do, you can fill me in. No," she protested when Carol started to speak, "that's it! I don't want to hear another word about Mr. Santee or his strange social habits. Let's eat, then if you have time you can show me around the gallery."

Carol, though obviously reluctant to leave such

a scintillating topic, wisely refrained from any further prodding. Carol's second favorite love was the van Buren Gallery. She genuinely liked her job and enjoyed talking about it, especially to Sloane, who had so much to learn about the art world and its keepers. Within seconds, she was off and running, Lucas Santee safely tucked away in a mental closet.

But it wasn't that easy for Sloane. Hard as she tried to concentrate on her friend's staccato commentary, her thoughts never strayed far from the bizarre incident and Santee's coldly hateful eyes, but she made a valiant effort to enjoy what was left of lunch and to look forward to the drive into Denver to visit the gallery.

Later, as the two women walked through the spacious art gallery, Sloane was enthralled with the opulence of it all. The painting and the sculpture were all of the highest quality, and there was a breathtaking display of Oriental porcelain, as well as a separate area showing some truly fine examples of silver work.

She was admiring a bracelet, a simple circlet with a delicate twisting design, when Carol said off-handedly, "Lucas bought Rena a lovely bracelet and ring for her sixteenth birthday. He was always spoiling her with expensive things. Poor Lucas."

And poor Rena.

All joy in the gallery and its treasures was ruined. First that unsettling encounter with Santee and now Carol's unknowing reminder of his sister's tragic death—her enthusiasm slipped away to be replaced by a growing depression.

As soon as she could without seeming rude, she ended the tour.

"I'd better be going, Carol. There are several things I need to pick up before I go home."

Carol looked at her cannily. "If you think I buy that excuse, dear heart, you're mistaken. Now what's with you and Lucas?"

Sloane shook her head firmly. "I'm not ready to talk about it yet, so be a friend and don't ask, okay?" Her head was beginning to throb with tension. "I'll call you in a couple of days."

"But I was going to introduce you to van Buren," Carol protested. "You've got to talk to him about the exhibit."

"Some other time. I'm just not up to it today. Thanks for lunch."

She left quickly before Carol could launch a counterattack. Carol's feelings were hurt at not being allowed to share the secret, she knew, but it couldn't be helped. Right now she needed to be alone, to think it out; she had to try to find a solution to the puzzle.

Thursday morning was chilly and gray, the northeasterly wind heavy with the promise of snow. Sloane was glad she'd decided to drive into Snowcrest today instead of waiting until Saturday as she usually did; another day or two might see her snowbound.

When she stopped for gas, Ernie Crow, who owned the only station in town, reminded her the car hadn't been "winterized." "Good thing you come by, Miz Taylor," he drawled in slow Alabaman, "we're in fer a real freeze by the weekend. Why, yore block might've froze up solid an' you'd a-been stuck 'thout no car."

"I know, Ernie. Guess I'm getting careless in my old age." She slid out of the car and handed him the keys. "You do whatever needs doing, and I'll be back after a while. I've only got a few errands to do, and the walk will do me good."

Ernie nodded energetically, his Adam's apple bobbing. "That's fine, Miz Taylor. She'll be ready by the time you git back."

Sloane set out across the square, her face raised to catch the moist, chilly current that whipped the ends of her hair around the red scarf that imprisoned it. She'd always thrived on natural turbulence; wind, rain, storms of all kinds seemed to energize and excite her.

Not that this was a storm, but it was a change from the unseasonable warmth, and she liked the way her skin tingled with the cold. She stretched her long legs out to their maximum stride, fairly bouncing around the hamlet to do her errands: a visit to the post office, where she couldn't help but be reminded of the day she'd met Santee and received the letter from Michael; next, a short stop at the general store for a few grocery staples; then on to Johanssen's for a chat with Margaret, who was thrilled at her news about the van Buren art exhibit.

"That's wonderful, Sloane! And you deserve it. You're the most talented artist we've had around here since Eva Pascal back in the early fifties."

Sloane laughed. "Has anyone ever told you what a great egobooster you are?"

"Not lately," Margaret quipped, "but I try. Oh! There's Lucas. I do hope he stops in. I haven't talked to him in—why, I guess it's been nearly a year."

Sloane involuntarily turned to follow Margaret's gaze out the front window. Santee's black pickup was passing slowly. Then it turned the corner to pull into Ernie Crow's station.

An unaccountable excitement rose in her, a thrill of anticipation that surprised her. After all, it wasn't as though he'd be glad to see her. He probably wouldn't even speak to her.

". . . went to high school with my son, and he was the nicest young man," Margaret was saying. "That's not surprising, though, with his upbringing. Some folks around here were a little upset when old Luke brought Rachel here as his bride. Back then feeling against Indians ran pretty high, like with all minority groups, I guess. But she was the loveliest thing, friendly and polite, but real sure of herself, too, if you know what I mean."

"I think so. She acted like everyone's equal, so you all had to accept her as one."

"Exactly. Rachel and I became very close, and I can truthfully say I never had a better friend. I stayed with her for a few days when Lucas' father died. She didn't show much to the ones who dropped by to pay their respects, but one night she broke down and cried for hours, all the time trying not to wake up the boy. She didn't want to upset him, she said. Oh, she was a fine lady. Why, by the time Lucas was born nobody around here even thought of her as an Indian anymore."

"It must have taken a lot of courage for her to leave her world and come to ours. She must have loved her husband very much."

"It was almost like a real romance, the kind you read. He had gone to New Mexico to buy some stock, and he met her there. She was a teacher on the reservation, one of the first Indian women to get any kind of higher education. Luke was devoted to her. I was glad she had Art Davidson, though, when Luke died. He was good to her and to Lucas. Between the three of them, they did a fine job of raising that boy. Do you know him?"

"Yes, we've met." She made a sudden decision. "Excuse me, Margaret, there's something I have to do. I'll see you next week, weather willing." And she headed for the door, her few parcels clutched tightly to her chest, leaving Margaret to stare after her in open-mouthed astonishment at her unusual abruptness.

As she crossed the street, her eyes fixed on Santee's imposing figure, her heart pounded with apprehension. Why on earth was she so bent on this confrontation? He'd made it more than plain his feelings toward her. And if he knew the whole *public* story, then she had to admit his resentment was justified. She didn't want to acknowledge why it was so important that he know the truth, only that he must.

Santee and Ernie were in conversation, their backs toward her when she approached them. She heard Santee's low rumble, in pleasant contrast to Ernie's somewhat nasal twang.

"That's a little beauty," Santee was saying, indicating the blue sports car.

"Yeah," Ernie agreed, "and Miz Taylor shore wears it nice."

"Taylor?" Santee grunted, sounding startled.

"In the flesh," Sloane interrupted. She enjoyed the look on Santee's dark face when he swung round to face her. "And thank you for the compliment, Ernie. Is the 'little beauty' ready?"

"Yep, all took care of. Here, lemme put them bags in the car fer you, then I'll total up the damages. Be right back with you, Luke."

Once Ernie was out of earshot, Sloane wasted no time on preliminaries. "I'd like to talk to you, Santee."

He turned those cold eyes on her, and she felt the full effect of their chill. "I don't think we have anything to discuss.'' He turned away, but she grabbed his arm.

"Well, I do. This thing between us—Santee, we've got to talk about it. I know how you feel, but . . .''

"If you knew how I feel, you'd drop the subject. Now.''

She shook her head in exasperation. "Santee, we live in the same town, we know the same people, and we'll be seeing each other all the time. If we can't be civil when we meet . . .''

He answered scathingly, "We've managed to avoid each other for the past two years until now. There's no reason why we can't go on the same way.'' He walked to his truck and opened the door, not looking back even once.

She watched him drive away and wanted to weep.

The cold contempt she'd seen in Santee's face haunted her throughout the rest of the day and into the night. She couldn't think; she couldn't work. For a while she doodled with sketches for several new projects she'd been considering, but somehow all the lines kept coming together in the same form—Santee's face. Strong planes, high cheekbones, a nose just a bit too broad-bridged for classical male beauty, hooded gray eyes that could melt or freeze at a glance. Eyes that accused.

It wasn't the first time she'd faced ugly, unspoken accusation. Three years ago, she'd seen a lot of it.

"Michael, I'm frightened. This has been going on for weeks, and it's getting worse."

"For God's sake, Sloane, must we go through all this again? The guy's a crank, he wants attention. When he doesn't get it, he'll stop." Michael turned from her to speak to a young man who sported a distinctive campaign button reading, "Fielding Works For YOU!"

"Excuse me, sir, but the first returns are coming in. And the news coordinator for Channel Eight is on line two."

"Thank you, Jerry. I'll be right there. Sloane, we can discuss this later, if you insist. But now, would it be asking too much for you to smile and *appear* to be supportive?"

Tears of frustration, all too familiar these past weeks, stung her eyes, and she bit back the impulse to spit something particularly nasty at Michael's departing back.

Campaign headquarters was crowded, the aides and workers, mostly college students, milling and scurrying about with end-of-the-trail enthusiasm. Few of them had thoughts for anyone other than their revered candidate, Michael Torrance Fielding. *How handsome he is,* whispered the coeds. *He'll make a wonderful state representative,* crowed the matrons. *He's in our pocket,* gloated the backers. Sloane knew what was said about her husband; for the most part, she agreed. He was handsome, he would be an excellent political leader, and he was crooked as a melted Tootsie Roll. But after five years, she had ceased to care. She would be free soon, free of Michael, free to leave Dallas and escape the frightening phone calls and notes.

"Hey, Sloane, how's it going? You've been scarce the past couple of days."

"Oh! Rena, you startled me. Yes, too many luncheons and cocktail parties, I suppose. I haven't felt up to par lately." She couldn't tell Rena it was fear keeping her at home, a spooky premonition of death and disaster that followed her like a shadow.

The younger woman looked at Sloane quizzically. "It wouldn't have anything to do with those crank calls you've been getting? Have you reported them to the police?"

"No, not yet. Michael seems to think the man will lose interest if he's ignored. And with the election and all, we didn't want it to get into the papers."

"Well, for what it's worth, I think you're right to be concerned. Your husband's a great politician, Sloane, but he falls a little short in the sensitivity department." She laughed gaily at Sloane's expression. "Don't look so surprised! Not *all* the campaign workers have a crush on the candidate. Anyway, I brought you this letter. Probably a late campaign contribution. Oops, Jerry's waving at me! Catch you later."

Watching Rena hurry away, Sloane smiled, enjoying her friend's youthful exuberance. Rena was a lovely young woman, a premed student, bright, and friendly. They had become quite close over the past months. In fact, Sloane had decided to take advantage of Rena's invitation to go home with her to Colorado during the Christmas holidays.

She turned the envelope over idly and lifted the flap. There was one sheet of paper inside and only three typed lines. It was unsigned. *"I held my own election. You lost. You should be nicer to your constituents. Watch for my election returns tonight."* She shivered. Another threat. Not explicit, but she felt the meaning. She was in grave danger from someone she didn't know, and she didn't have the slightest idea why. All the messages were like that, implying she had done something to this unknown man. *"Watch for my election returns tonight."*

Sloane was icy with fear.

She found Michael in the television room, surrounded by excited supporters who cheered as the returns flashed on the screen. "Michael, I got another letter . . ."

"I'm glad you're here, darling," he interrupted. "Gloria just called. She's finished the revisions on my acceptance speech. I told her you'd drive over and pick it up."

She couldn't believe it. "Michael, you aren't even listening to me. I just got another threat. Someone is out there waiting for me, and you want to send me out this late to pick up your speech! I want to call the police—now!''

He scowled and pulled her into a corner. "Please don't make another scene, Sloane. You've got to remember we're very much in the public eye right now."

"Blast your public! I'm being threatened, Michael, and I'm afraid! I want the police called in on this. I want your support."

Michael took the letter from her and read it slowly. "I see no threat in this, Sloane. As usual you're overreacting . . ."

"No! I *know* this, Michael. I feel it! He is out there, waiting for me!" She snatched the sheet of paper from his hand. "I'm going to call the police. Pick up your own speech and stuff it!"

A few moments later, as she was waiting for a free phone line, Rena approached her. "Sloane, may I borrow your coat? I've spilled coffee all down the front of mine."

"Sure. And there's a scarf in the pocket," Sloane replied absently, beginning to punch in the number of police dispatch.

"Thanks, love. By the way, I heard from my brother. He says he'd love to have you visit with us during Christmas. See ya."

A harried voice answered on the third ring, and Sloane was only peripherally aware of Rena taking Sloane's navy blue coat off the rack, of Rena leaving the building, taking Sloane's car keys from the pocket of the coat, of Michael speaking to

Rena as she went out the door. "Yes, this is Sloane Fielding. I'd like to speak to an officer, please."

Then it clicked. She dropped the receiver and grabbed Michael's arm as he walked past. "Where's Rena going?" she demanded, unable to control the trembling of her voice.

"To Gloria's."

She was out the door and in the alley before she was even conscious of the movement. Beside the sedan parked close to the building, barely visible in the dim light cast by the street lamp, a crumpled figure lay, looking like someone's discarded laundry. A terrible pain rose up, ripping through her mind, and she screamed.

Much later a reporter cornered her inside. "Mrs. Fielding, is it true Rena Davidson was murdered by mistake, that *you* were the intended victim?"

She had expected that question sooner or later. Too many people had heard her quarrel with Michael; someone was bound to mention it. "I have no comment."

But the eager young man wasn't through. His next question staggered her. "Mrs. Fielding, your husband stated Miss Davidson left the building to run an errand for you. Would you care to comment on why you sent her out in your coat, to your car, when by your own admission, you were convinced someone was waiting out there to harm you?"

She didn't—couldn't—answer. The accusation hung there like a barrier between her and the now-silent onlookers. The reporter pressed his advantage.

"Is it true you received an anonymous threat only moments before you sent Miss Davidson to pick up a copy of your husband's speech?"

"Before *I* sent her . . . ?" Her throat was dry and sore and she could only whisper the words clamoring in her head.

"Yes, Mr. Fielding stated . . ."

Sloane turned her head slowly, searching for Michael in the crowded room. He was there, not more than ten feet away, yet she seemed to see him at a great distance. Their eyes met for the briefest moment, then he looked away. But she had seen what she was afraid of seeing. She was to be the scapegoat, the campaign sacrifice.

A rising wind rustled through the trees surrounding the cabin, rousing her to a cold and dark early morning. Sunday's forecast of colder weather had been accurate if a trifle premature. The cold front had held off until now, but it threatened to make up for its tardiness with intensity. Already the temperature inside was perceptibly lower.

Shrugging into a jacket, she stepped out the back door to the woodpile, being careful to prop open the door while she made several trips to stack the short logs beside the fireplace. In a way the automatic locks on the doors were a blessing, but it could be disastrous to be shut out accidentally. She'd made that mistake once and found there was absolutely no way to gain entrance without a key. It had taken a locksmith and a small fortune to get back inside.

Her wood gathered, she sat curled up on a floor pillow and cradled a warm mug of chocolate between her palms as she watched the darting flames. She was weary, confused, worried, and more than a little angry. It had been a long time since she expected life to be fair, but at least it should be willing to compromise now and then.

What was Santee's hold on her, the reason for her aching sadness? Could simple attraction account for that deep sense of loss gnawing at her belly? No, there was more to it than that, much more. Something in her responded to the mere face of his *being*, existing in the same world, an indescribable *rightness*. Kismet. Was that the right word? Whatever the philosophical definition, she was attuned to Santee's emotions and thoughts to a disturbing degree. His grief for Rena, his impotent anger over the unfairness of her death, and then the shock of her own connection with that tragedy—how confused and hurt he must be right now.

Should she make the first move or wait to see if he would contact her? Logic told her to let it slide, that a meeting now, given his attitude, would resolve nothing. And wouldn't it be better if the relationship ended now, before it started? Even if all the other problems were worked out, she could never give him a family—the thing she sensed was most important to him. But logic overlooked the emotional reality. Already he meant too much to her.

She made her decision. Santee had twenty-four hours in which to come to her. Then she would do it her way.

Chapter Three

SANTEE STOOD LEANING against the stall door, watching the foal nuzzle its mother, greedy and awkward in its newness, eager to gain its footing in an unfamiliar world. It had been a difficult birth for Cinnamon this time, a strenuous twelve hours for both mare and rancher, and Santee was exhausted. As soon as he was sure the chestnut and her foal were okay, he could hit the shower and the breakfast table. He ached for the comfort of the big bed upstairs, but that would have to wait. Until Hank could throw away his crutches, Santee had double duty around the ranch.

As he watched, the foal's legs buckled, tumbling the still-damp animal into a most undignified heap. Then, plucky to the core, he regained his balance. A beautiful, sound animal, thought Santee; maybe he should be kept for breeding instead of being sold. His sire, Old Jet, was prime stock and the young'un appeared to have bred true, with the same lines and coloring, a deep, lustrous brown that was almost black . . .

Into his mind's eye slipped the image of a woman with brown-black hair falling in soft waves, brown eyes sparkling with humor, a soft, generous mouth he'd longed to taste.

"Damn!" The thud of his boot against a post startled the mare and she shifted uncomfortably.

Sloane Taylor. He still couldn't believe she'd had the nerve to show up here. Did she think no one would care, that *he* wouldn't care? Or maybe she thought because he hadn't been there when Rena died he didn't have all the facts. But he did. He knew everything he needed to know. The newspapers had carried detailed reports on Rena's death, and the facts were clear. Through criminal negligence, Sloane Taylor had caused Rena's death by sending her out into a situation Sloane herself was afraid to face. According to statements from two of the campaign workers who had been present that night, Sloane had given her coat to Rena, then calmly made a telephone call while Rena walked out the door to her death. Even her own husband had implicated her. Sure, Fielding had later retracted his statement, but that was only what any concerned husband would have done.

The only thing missing was the official police report, and he doubted it could have added anything.

No, it was too clear and too incredible. His sister was dead in *her* place, and she apparently wanted him to ignore the situation. *No way, lady. Just stay out of my way, and I'll stay out of yours.* He shook his head and ran his fingers through thick black hair, tangled from the hours of hard work and sleeplessness.

He remembered when he'd first seen her, fear stamped on her pale face; he'd wanted to hold and protect her. Later, he'd wanted to hold her again, to touch that soft flesh, bury himself in her. The urgency of his desire had both surprised and pleased him. But now it sickened him, for he was very much afraid he'd feel the same way if she were here now, even knowing who and what she was.

The drive to Santee's ranch took just over half an hour, time enough for her to come to the brink of turning back more than once. It would have been so easy to go back home; she wasn't looking forward to this meeting. But neither did she relish the prospect of spending yet another day and night on tenterhooks, waiting for the phone to ring, expecting to hear his truck turn in to her driveway. No, his twenty-four hours were up, and she would keep her promise to herself to beard the lion in his den.

Dogged determination had brought her as far as

the main gate. She stopped the blue Celica and sat looking at the sign: *Crooked Creek Ranch—Saddle Horses*. This was it—she could still turn back and keep her easy, uncomplicated solitude, her hard won independence. But she wouldn't.

She pressed the accelerator and shot through the gate.

Along the half-mile drive to the main house, she thought she'd never seen a lovelier place than Santee's valley. Gently sloping pasture land, touched now with frost, reached up into the thickly forested hillsides and were dotted here and there with cattle. Nearer, two gangly colts danced circles around a mare, kicking their heels and shaking their manes in enthusiastic abandonment. She watched other fine horses prancing and cavorting behind the high fences, obviously invigorated by the crisp, chill weather. In the distance Mt. Evans stood sentinel, white-crested and stately. All around her were sights and sounds of a smoothly run, well-ordered universe that contrasted sharply with her inner turmoil.

The gravel road led to a large house, two-storied and obviously not new but well tended and sturdy, a house that had been lived in and loved. Perhaps a hundred yards beyond, to the east and slightly behind the house, was a long low building that she took to be the stables. As the car rolled to a gentle stop and she switched off the engine, a man appeared at the door of the outbuilding. She took a deep breath and got out, nervously brushing her long hair away from her face. Santee.

His face was set in the expression she remembered from the restaurant. His mouth, once so soft and sensual when he looked at her, was now drawn in a grim straight line above the rock-hard jaw. His eyes glinted dangerously and he clenched one fist compulsively before striding forward.

"Hello, Santee." Her voice was soft and appealing, with a note of pleading that he either did not hear or chose to ignore.

"You weren't invited here."

"I know. But I need to talk to you."

He turned his back to her, and she thought he would simply walk away, leaving her standing alone to talk to the wind that was beginning to blow her hair across her face. But he turned abruptly.

Instinctively she stepped backward, away from what she saw reflected in his face. He saw the alarm in her eyes and laughed mockingly. "You're right to be afraid of me. Is that what you want to talk about?" he challenged.

She accepted the gauntlet. "Yes, I suppose it is. I know now about your relationship with Rena. And I'm more sorry than I can say to be the one to remind you of her death."

"Remind me?" He spoke in an ominously low voice, almost a whisper. The pulse in his neck beat visibly, throbbing out in rage. "Do you really think that's all? Did you think that once I found out who you were, I wouldn't care? Or maybe you thought I wouldn't find out. Is that it? You thought you could go on with your little charade indefinitely?''

The more he spoke, the more nervous she became. ''No!'' she protested. ''I wasn't trying to hide anything. If I'd known who you were, I'd have spoken before now. I *want* to tell you about it. That's why I'm here.''

''You're here on the ranch to try and convince me you weren't responsible for my sister's murder. I haven't figured out why you're in Colorado. Morbid curiosity? Or did you think because Rena died in your place, you could take her place here and get rid of your guilt? Forget it, *Mrs. Fielding!*''

The rage and pain he emanated hit her like a gale, and she reeled from the impact. ''Santee, I don't know exactly what you've heard, but I do know what you haven't heard . . .''

''I've heard it all. In case you've forgotten, the newspapers gave you quite a write-up!''

''You should know newspapers don't always report everything. There's a lot more to the story, so stop shouting at me so we can talk.'' She fought back tears of frustration while she frantically searched for the right words, words that would make him listen.

His gut tightened as he watched her. He felt suffocated by the situation, hating and wanting her with equal intensity. His control was crumbling and when it snapped he wasn't sure which way it would go. Either way, it would be ugly. He had to make her leave.

"Tears won't work, either," he snarled. "Rena wrote me about you. She said you were her friend, you were 'nice' to her. So 'nice' you sent her out to face a lunatic and now she's dead!"

"Santee, please listen . . ."

"No! You can't say anything I want to hear! Now get off my land and don't come back or, by God, the next time I just may break your neck!" He turned on his heel and walked quickly into the stables.

Stunned by the venom and violence of his words, Sloane stood for a moment before mustering the courage to follow him inside. Reason told her to leave, to run from the danger, but instinct prompted her to try once more to reach him.

The light in the stables was much dimmer than the outside brightness, and it took her eyes a few moments to adjust. Then she saw him at the far stall, one foot propped on the bottom slat of the gate, his arms resting on the top board as he gazed unseeing at a mare who was contentedly nuzzling a foal that couldn't have been more than a few hours old. Looking at him lost in pain, her heart ached for his loss, for his misery, and most of all for the chasm that threatened to swallow up their relationship before it had a chance to grow into the beautiful thing she knew it could be.

"Santee."

He swung round. "What the hell does it take to get through to you? I don't want you here!"

She stepped toward him impulsively, her hands held out in supplication. "Please listen to me. When we first met, there was something magic between us, a bond. It was as if we'd known each other forever. And you felt it, too; I know you did. Remembering that, can you honestly think me capable of putting Rena in danger? I loved her. She was my friend."

His laugh mocked her. "A 'magic bond'? Is that what they call it now? I call it sex appeal, chemistry, or any one of a dozen other things. I don't deny the *attraction*," he sneered, raking his eyes over her in a manner calculated to insult. "But don't glorify what was nothing more than a momentary urge. What I felt for you that day has nothing to do with the kind of person you are."

Seeing behind his bitterness, she was calm when she replied. "You don't really mean that, Santee."

"Do you need proof?" In two angry strides, he was beside her, his hands gripping her arms painfully as he pulled her against his hard body, his mouth trapping hers in a brutal, demeaning kiss that held nothing but contempt and a desire to degrade and humiliate her. There was pain in the soft inner tissue of her lips and in the flesh of her upper arms where he held her with bruising intensity.

The assault, for there was no other word for it, caught her off guard; for a moment she made no response other than a choked cry and a stiffening of her body. Then anger and fear took over, and she began to fight, trying to twist away from the ruthless punishment of his mouth. But as her hands pressed ineffectively against the rock hard muscles of his chest, the buttons of his shirt slipped loose; instead of fabric, she felt the crisply curling hair, the warmth of his skin. A heady aroma of hay and sweat and man triggered a frightening explosion of passion within her.

In that moment Santee knew he was lost. A tender warmth unfolded in his mind, then reached out to touch her. His lips softened and parted, coaxing hers to do the same, both seeking and promising pleasure. His arms slipped around her, pressing so tightly she was breathless, while his lips left hers to explore the tenderness of her neck, the hollow of her throat.

It could have been hours later or merely seconds, so tightly woven was their web when the embrace was broken. Floating in sensation, she looked into his face and saw only love and need; gently, lovingly, she traced his lips with her finger and breathed his name: "Santee."

The sound of her voice broke the spell. He was suddenly still, looking at her through the eyes of a distant stranger, appalled by his self-betrayal. And still he wanted her.

Filled with loathing, he pushed her away. "Be very sure this is what you want, Miss Taylor, before I take you here in the dirt."

His dark, brooding face, only inches above her own, was suddenly menacing; his abrupt withdrawal left her icy with fear. For a moment, shock left her disoriented. "What?" she whispered, filled with emptiness. "I thought . . ."

"You thought this would change things? You're responsible for my sister's death. That will never change."

She pulled away from him, for his hands still grasped her shoulders, warm and soft and deceiving. "You're wrong about me, Santee. When you figure it out—and you will—you'll come to me."

If he had looked closely, he'd have seen the unsteadiness in her legs, the tremor that shook her hands while she straightened her clothing. But through the haze of mingled rage and shame, he saw nothing but the strong set of her shoulders and the proud tilt of her head.

Behind her, she heard the thwack of his fist hitting something solid as she walked away.

Once through the gate and off the Crooked Creek property, she pulled the car over to the side of the narrow gravel road. She should have seen it coming, she thought; she *did* see it coming but chose to ignore the warnings. How could she have so misjudged her ability to break through his defenses? Mind-link aside, that experience was too degrading, too painful, to be repeated. She meant what she had said; she was through making the first move. From now on it was up to him.

Wearily, she rested her head against the steering wheel. *Too much too soon. I'm tired of coping. All I want to do is cry.* When the tears came, she thought they would go on forever. She sat in the car, so very alone, and cried in great sobs that left her drained. Then she wiped away the tears with the heel of her hand and drove home.

This part of Dallas was well manicured and exclusive. He had to be very careful to stay out of sight; strangers were noticed in places like this. Nothing but a bunch of hysterical fools, most of them, guarding their precious property from contamination by the lower class. If he had time, he'd leave his calling card for a few of them—stupid fools. Thought they were better than everybody else.

But he had to be careful now. This was his last shot. He'd been watching the house off and on for several weeks, but had never seen her going in or out, only that whey-faced cow who worked there. It seemed that prissy Mrs. Fielding had moved away. Did she really think it would be that easy, that she could just walk away from the punishment she deserved?

No. He'd promised to make her pay, and he

always kept his promises. He would find her and make her sorry for the way she'd treated him, no matter how far she had run. There was nothing he couldn't do, no one he couldn't find; his power was limitless. He had always paid back the people who had scorned him, and she would be no different.

Just hang in there, Mrs. Fielding. I'll be seein' you real soon.

Chapter Four

THE LOFT OF the cabin had originally been one large bedroom with an adjoining bath and a sun deck accessible through large sliding-glass doors. When Sloane had decided to work at home, it had seemed both practical and desirable to partition off a small section of the loft as a sleeping area and convert the rest into a studio, with her main work table near the deck to catch the best light. She had also installed a skylight which, coupled with the natural light from the cathedral windows in the front of the house, gave the upstairs studio a delightfully airy feel. It had proven to be a wise piece of renovation, for she had done her best work in the two years since. And best of all, she could still sit on the deck in the early mornings and watch the sun rise through the trees.

During the spring and summer birds of all varieties busily fed, mated, and raised their young, all within sight and sound; and other animals, too, entertained her for hours on end, scampering and scolding. Until lately she had never felt the need to share this place with anyone.

But now she was acutely aware of a new feeling, a sort of empty ache that she reluctantly identified as loneliness. She could picture a man sitting on the deck with her, a tall, brooding man whose face would light up in an instant as she pointed out the eccentric habits of the family of squirrels who lived in the tree not twenty feet away from her bedroom. The brilliance of a pink and gold sunrise early on an October morning would be doubly glorious if shared with him.

She had watched the sun come up this morning, as she had so many times before, trying to recapture the serenity that had always been as near as the view from her window. But today the magic was dulled by the memory of her ugly encounter with Santee. The intensity of her attraction to him was so hard to fathom; she had only just met him. Certainly she couldn't claim to know him, at least not in the traditional sense, and he had hurt and humiliated her beyond bearing. Then why this sense of loss, this desolation? Why couldn't she put it aside, the way she'd always handled her private pain?

You're being silly and childish, she scolded. *Worrying won't change things. If Santee and I are meant to be together, it will happen. If the karma is right.*

If. The biggest word in the language. If Michael hadn't decided to build a pool house that summer nearly four years ago, she wouldn't even be here right now.

Ifs were endless. Once you started tracing them, they went on forever, and she simply didn't have time for them now. She had a past to escape, a man to forget, and a career to build, starting now. *If* she could put Santee out of her mind long enough to pick up her chisel . . .

For the rest of the day and deep into the night, she set a frantic pace for herself, finding only a mild antidote in hard work. The shaggy buffalo, the largest piece she'd ever attempted, began to look downright ragged as the chisel chipped away at the soft pine, so she abandoned it and tried polishing a few of her finished pieces. That, she discovered, didn't require enough concentration, so she moved to the sketch book. That effort fared no better than the rest.

When, at four o'clock the next morning, she noticed she was shaping a lump of clay into a reasonable facsimile of Santee's head, right down to the small cleft in his chin, she conceded defeat and fell into bed.

By ten o'clock, she was awake if not alert. At least, she comforted herself, the brief respite had served to give her a more objective outlook.

Santee's head, that product of her betraying subconscious, was more than an exercise in futility. In fact, she admitted objectively, it had real strength of character. Handled properly, maybe in wood, it would be a powerful piece for the exhibit, well worth the extra hours she would have to put in to finish it in time. *I'll do it,* she decided, *my own private rite of exorcism.*

She had just started smoothing out the preliminary clay model when she heard a car approach, and a few minutes later, the rattle of a key in the lock.

Carol opened the door and announced herself. "It's only me. I decided that if I waited for an invitation, I'd be too old to make the trip."

"I'm in the studio. Come on up." Sloane hoped she didn't sound as surprised as she felt. Carol had only been to the cabin three or four times, claiming "all that unbounded nature" made her sneeze. She much preferred entertaining Sloane in her fashionable Denver apartment or in restaurants and theaters.

Her stiletto heels clicked on the hardwood stairs as she grumbled, "You must be part pigeon, always wanting to roost at the top of the house. The eccentricity of genius, no doubt." When she walked into the studio she blinked in astonishment. "I *knew* something was wrong! Sloane, you look ghastly!"

"Thanks a lot." Sloane smiled wryly. "Did you drive all the way out here just to turn my head with flattery?" Actually she had been appalled at her own reflection in the dressing table mirror that morning. Dark circles made her eyes look larger than ever and told their tale about the sleepless night she had spent in her studio, taking out her frustrations on an innocent piece of clay.

"Don't be snitty," Carol snapped. "It isn't at all becoming." Then, more serious than Sloane had ever seen her, she continued. "Darling, I'm worried about you. I haven't heard from you since lunch the other day. And it's obvious you haven't been sleeping; you're about to drop where you stand. Not to mention the hollows of your cheeks—when's the last time you ate?" She touched Sloane's shoulder gently. "In case I've never said so, I care about you. Something's dreadfully wrong, and I'd like to help if I can."

Sloane rubbed at the stinging behind her eyelids with fingers that weren't quite steady. Funny how she reacted to sympathy—as long as she kept her problems to herself, she could cope, but one kind word could destroy all her defenses and leave her in tears.

"I appreciate your concern, Carol, I really do. But there's nothing you can do. It's something I have to work through for myself."

Plopping down on the bed, Carol looked discerningly at her friend. "It wouldn't have anything to do with Lucas, would it? Or those hints of your unsavory past that are going around town?" Sloane's stricken expression told Carol she was on target. "That's what I thought. It might help to talk about it. Contrary to public image, I'm a pretty good listener. And I'd like to hear your version.''

Sloane stared down at her trembling hands. ''I guess I should have expected him to tell someone, but somehow I didn't . . .''

''If by *him* you mean Lucas, I don't think he's said anything. Margaret Johanssen called me last night, and she was pretty upset. Apparently one of Lucas' hands heard you two arguing—about Rena.'' She took a deep breath. ''He said you had something to do with her death. In fact, he said you were responsible.''

''No! That's not true! I didn't know until too late . . .'' Too tired and weak to stand, Sloane sat beside Carol on the bed and sank her face into her hands. ''When I left Dallas, I thought it was all behind me—the ugliness, the accusations. I thought I could start over and forget it all.''

''Forget what?'' Carol whispered.

''Rena, Chapman—everything. She worked on Michael's campaign staff, you know. We were friends. She'd even invited me to go home with her for Christmas that year.'' She turned to Carol and took her hand. ''Are you sure you want to hear this?''

''I'm sure. What happened, Sloane? The whole story.''

''She was murdered by a man named Gerald Chapman. It was dark; she was wearing my coat, unlocking the door to my car. He didn't know it was Rena. He thought it was me, so he cut her throat.''

Carol's face, ash white, reflected her horror. "*Why?* Why you?"

Sloane shook her head helplessly. "At the time, I didn't know. I'd been getting anonymous calls and letters for several weeks, but I had no idea why, or who he was. Later, after he was caught, I recognized him.''

She stood abruptly and paced to the work table and back. "The summer before, Michael had decided to have a pool house built. There were four or five workmen on the grounds every day. Chapman was one of them.''

When she paused, Carol rummaged in her purse for a cigarette, lit it, and inhaled deeply. "Just an average Joe, indulging in the American work ethic, huh?''

Sloane managed a pale smile. "He seemed to be. I didn't know then, you see.'' She turned her back to Carol and gazed unseeing through the deck door. Her voice, when she spoke again, was faint but clear. "The first time I really noticed him, he was standing on the patio, looking into the den. He wasn't *doing* anything, just—looking. When I stepped into the room, he watched me with a sort of blank stare, like he was seeing something else. Then he walked away. A few days later, I came downstairs into Michael's study and Chapman was there. Michael had a picture of me in a small silver frame; he kept it on his desk. Chapman was holding it, staring at it. He heard me come in, but he barely glanced up, he just kept *standing* there with that picture. After a few seconds, I asked if I could help him, if he were looking for something. He stared at me for a minute, then he said, 'No, thanks.' He started to leave, but he looked at me again and said, 'You're a pretty lady.' Then he walked out.''

"What did Michael say when you told him?"

Sloane shrugged. "He said he'd speak to the job foreman, but he didn't, not then. Two days later, I found Chapman in my bedroom, watching me get out of the shower."

"Oh my God! What happened?" Carol sprang from the bed and gripped Sloane's arm, swinging her around. "Did he . . . ?"

"No. He didn't touch me. In fact, there was never anything overtly sexual in his attitude, only a kind of low-key menace. I screamed when I saw him. He didn't even react. He just stood there for a second or two, then he smiled and left. This time, Michael went to the foreman and Chapman was fired."

"So what happened?"

"For more than a year, nothing." Sloane was calmer now. Both she and Carol seated themselves on the bed again. Carol lit another cigarette.

"When I started getting the calls and letters, right after Michael and I had appeared on several local television shows, we thought it was just a crank, you know the kind. Anyone in the public

eye is fair game. But I was uneasy, I had a feeling
. . ." No, she couldn't tell Carol about the "feeling," the fear that had crept up her spine to make
her hair stand on end, the nightmares of being
pursued by an invisible horror. "Anyway, I insisted
Michael call the police. He refused. It would have
been bad for the campaign, he said. Finally, that
night . . ." She shivered.

Carol hugged her. "Come on, honey, we don't
have to talk about it anymore. I didn't realize . . ."

"No, I've got to finish it. That night, another
letter was delivered to me at campaign headquarters. I was so frightened, Carol, and Michael
wouldn't listen to me. The note said 'tonight,' and
Michael wanted me to drive across town, alone, to
pick up a copy of his speech!"

In the sudden silence, both women could hear
the steady ticking of the alarm clock on the bedside table.

Carol spoke first. "The rat," she whispered.

"Yes," Sloane responded mildly. "We quarreled, loudly. I told him what he could do with his
speech and went to call the police myself. While I
was on the phone, Rena asked if she could borrow
my coat. By the time I figured out what was
happening, it was too late. She was dead." The
tears were falling now, as though she were too
tired to hold them back any longer. "I found her
in the alley, beside my car."

Carol was crying, too. "I can't believe this is
real. And I still don't understand. How could any-

one say you were responsible? And what did you mean by 'accusations'?''

Sloane wiped her face. "Michael thought he was going to be elected state representative that night. He didn't want his almighty public to know he'd ignored all the warning signs and sent a young, helpless woman into the night to face a killer. There would have been a scandal."

Carol closed her eyes and moaned. "So it was easy to shift the blame to you. You loaned her the coat. Was that the official story? You were afraid to go out, so you sent her instead?" Another piece clicked into place and her eyes widened. "And that's what Lucas believes? Damn, damn!" She held Sloane tightly, stroking her hair. "Why did you move to Snowcrest, honey? He was bound to find out sooner or later."

"Rena talked about Snowcrest so often. She really loved the town and the people. In a way, I came to love it, too. I thought I could be happy here. And I didn't know Santee was her brother until you told me. I thought his name would be Davidson." She pulled away from her friend and stood up. "I went to see him, tried to explain, but he wouldn't even listen. He hates me, Carol, and I can't stand it!"

"I'll talk to him."

"No! You're not to say one word, to him or anyone else. You're my friend and I love you, but it's not your problem."

Carol reluctantly agreed. "All right, pet, if you

feel that strongly about it. But I think you're wrong. This is tearing you apart, and if you won't defend yourself . . .''

"No, Carol, I'll handle it myself."

"Okay, I'll hush. And go away. I've got a jillion questions, but you need some time alone to rest. Can I do anything before I leave?"

"Just promise to come back soon. And thanks."

By the time she heard Carol drive away, she had laid her head on a pillow and was drifting off to sleep. Vaguely she wondered why she didn't tell Carol all of it, about her role in Chapman's capture, his threats at the trial, his recent release? And about her psi abilities? She decided there were some things better left unsaid.

Next morning she awoke with new determination and energy. Her talk with Carol and a long, dreamless sleep had purged her of much of the emotional tension that had kept her on the edge of frenzy the past few days.

Outside it was sunny, although very cold, and the air seemed to sparkle with winter's promise. Unable to resist the prospect of what could be her last walk before the predicted snowfall made it too dangerous, she ate breakfast hurriedly, then pulled on jeans, a heavy cable knit sweater, and knee boots. A fur cap pulled down over her ears, some protective gloss on her lips and cheeks, and she was ready.

She struck off briskly through the trees to the

east of her cabin, knowing precisely where she wanted to go. The smell of spruce was sharp and clear, bringing back memories of the first time she had seen the cabin, the unmistakable welcome of the surrounding forest. Coming straight from a small one-bedroom apartment in Denver where she had been surrounded on all sides by other tenants, the openness and solitude here were irresistibly attractive. Although her city neighbors were not intrusive, being too wrapped up in their own pursuits to be interested in Sloane Taylor's personal problems, still their very proximity threatened her need for privacy and an uncluttered space where time and serenity could start the healing process.

She hadn't intended to live in Colorado at all. After the trial, the impulse to run away had become too strong to resist, so she packed two suitcases, loaded them in her car and started driving. Somewhere around Amarillo, she decided to go to Snowcrest to see where Rena had grown up. When she saw the Rockies for the first time, the magic of the mountains had taken over. Denver was the logical choice because she needed to find a job, to stay busy. But Michael was very generous with the divorce settlement, and she soon realized she could live anywhere she wanted.

When she first mentioned it to Carol, whom she had met at the gallery, her new friend had been incredulous that anyone would want to leave the city bustle for small-town boredom. She could still remember Carol's words: "Personally, dear, I think you're playing with a short deck; but if you're serious, I know just the man for you. He handles a lot of that back-to-nature idiocy. Only last week he was telling me about a place that's just come on the market in Snowcrest."

Looking back, she could almost believe fate had directed her to this retreat. She had never regretted her decision. It was here she had come back to life.

She walked all the way to the crest overlooking the valley and rested there for nearly an hour, drinking in the beauty of the panorama spread for miles below. Perched on a flat rock, she watched toy cars glide noiselessly on a tiny ribbon of highway surrounded by dots of houses and livestock, while almost at eye level hawks wheeled and dived and swooped through the crystal clarity of a pale blue sky.

At last, recharged, she hiked back to the cabin, fortified, at least temporarily, with balance and order.

As she emerged from the trees beside the cabin, she saw a tan station wagon parked beside her car. For a moment she couldn't make the connection and her heart began to hammer in alarm. She had very few visitors, and she couldn't help the surge of apprehension at the sight of the strange vehicle. As she drew nearer she could see someone sitting in the car, a man. He turned his head and looked directly at her, his expression unreadable. Lucas Santee.

Her pulses beat a tattoo. Had she somehow conjured him up with her daydreaming? No, of course not, how childish. But she remembered the rage in his face the last time they'd met, the barely controlled violence. Should she be afraid of him? Despite her feelings, she really didn't know what he might be capable of under stress, and stress seemed to be the major ingredient in their relationship.

He opened the door and got out, his long legs covering the distance between them in a few strides.

"I've been waiting for you."

"I can tell. How did you find me?"

"Carol. I called her last night. We have to talk."

How ironic. He'd been on her mind constantly and now that he was there, she was afraid to be alone with him. And it was more than concern for her safety. He had debased and humiliated her. She had more than a right to be angry with him, but already the anger was dissipating. Instead she was remembering how right, how complete, she had felt in his arms, and that memory was awesomely dangerous.

"We could have talked on the phone. I'm sure Carol would have given you my number."

"She did. But I didn't want you hanging up on me."

"And I don't want you dropping in on me. Please leave." She turned her back on him and walked to the cabin door.

He was close behind her, stubbornness in the set of his body. "Look, I know you're angry with me. I'm sorry for what happened the other day. But I came to say something, and I want you to listen!"

She wheeled around to face him, brown eyes blazing. "Well, that's a typical remark. You want me to listen? Like you listened to me? I don't think so, Santee. I don't care for your brand of conversation."

She knew he was going to touch her before it happened. It was what she'd been trying to avoid, but she had barely fitted key to lock when he took her arm in a steel grip.

"More caveman tactics, Santee? Don't you have an alternate approach?"

His hand dropped. "I'm sorry. But this is important to me. I just want to talk to you."

"Can't it wait a few days, just until we're both a little more in control? You're angry, I'm angry. I really don't want to see you right now."

"It won't take long. I want to know about Rena, about her life before. . . . I didn't see her after she left home. I'd like you to tell me about her."

Their gazes held for a long moment, then she sighed. "All right. But we keep the kitchen table between us."

His mouth twitched briefly. "Agreed."

In only a few minutes, they were seated at the glass and chrome table with mugs of steaming coffee creating a misty barrier between them. She looked at him guardedly, still a bit uneasy. What if he touched her again? She knew she would welcome his embrace, knew too that another encounter now would end as badly as the last one.

"What do you want to know?"

"Everything." His tortured eyes pleaded wordlessly.

She closed her eyes for a moment, picturing Rena's lovely young face, the way she almost skipped when she walked. "Rena was so special. She was friendly and hard working. Everyone loved her."

"Not everyone."

She hurried past that pitfall. "She was involved in a student group on campus—that's how she came to work for Michael. Before she could start changing the world, she said, she wanted to find out how the machinery worked."

He almost smiled. "That sounds like her. What about her friends? In one of her letters, she mentioned a boy. She wanted me to meet him."

"That was probably Toby." Sloane smiled, remembering the skinny young man and his puppylike devotion to Rena. "They were almost inseparable. They had talked about getting married when they finished school."

"And now she'll never do any of the things she dreamed about." His face was ugly with suppressed emotion. "Because of Chapman—and you. Neither one of you has ever really paid for that."

"Oh, not again! Look, I'm trying to be cooperative, Santee, but you're making it awfully hard—for both of us. Obviously your mind's made up about me, so I won't waste my breath trying to reason with you. And I won't sit here and be abused again.'' Fighting to contain her rapidly rising temper, she looked at him squarely. ''I'm willing to talk with you about Rena, but that's it. If you want to fight, go somewhere else.''

His mug banged onto the table, splashing black coffee over the pristine surface. ''Don't you feel anything? Rena was barely twenty years old; she hadn't even started to live; and she was *butchered!*''

His pain was a palpable thing in the room, invading her space. He needed comforting, but she knew he wouldn't accept it from her.

''It's over, Santee. She's gone. Beating yourself, and me, with it won't bring her back.''

He glared at her darkly. ''Who the hell are you to be telling me how to deal with my grief? She was my sister, the only family I had. There was no sense to her death. It should have been *you!*'' Standing abruptly, he pushed the chair noisily across the floor and strode around the table. ''You're only mouthing platitudes with no meaning.''

''I will *not* let you push me into another scene.'' She rose from the table, hanging on to her composure by a thin thread. She felt too deeply for him, experienced too much of his pain. Overlaying that was her own hurt, frustration, and outrage at his accusations. ''Whether you believe me or not, I *do* know what you're feeling. And I also know the difference between healthy grief and destructive obsession. You're hurting yourself, and you're trying to punish me for something I didn't do.''

His face registered incredulity, then fury. ''You're unbelievable! How can you deny it? Your own husband said you sent Rena out that night.''

''He lied.''

''What about the others? Did they lie, too?''

''What others? You never *tell* me what you've heard, so how can I answer you?''

''You can't answer me. That's the real truth, isn't it? My first impression of you was right. You're a cold, manipulative . . .''

''Wrong, cowboy,'' she spat, goaded beyond endurance. ''That was your *second* opinion of me. Now, if you've got what you wanted, why don't you get out?''

''I'm not sure what I wanted,'' he muttered thickly, pulling her firmly into his arms, so quickly she didn't have time to protest.

There was no gentleness in his kiss or in his embrace, which pinned her against his lean, hard body. It was a savage possession, rekindling the hurt he'd inflicted on her before; she began to fight him. She barely felt the bruising of his lips and hands, intent only on escaping. With fear-induced strength she wrenched away from him, gasping for breath.

''What is it with you?'' she demanded. ''If you hate me so much, why can't you keep your hands to yourself?''

"Hell, I don't know! I think I've lost my mind." He stepped back, turning away from her. "This whole thing is driving me crazy. I know what you are, what you've done, but still . . ."

"Can't kick the 'chemistry,' huh?" she taunted. "Oh, I can understand that much. But there are more socially acceptable ways of satisfying your urges."

He still wouldn't face her. "You'll just have to take my word that rape isn't my usual method."

"No, I don't think it is. I remember the day we met, when you were a different person." Her anger had cooled, and she was no longer afraid of him.

He turned, started to speak, but she continued. "You hate me but you want me. And you hate yourself for wanting me. So you try to hurt both of us. It's not right—I can't even tell you I think it's normal under the circumstances. But it is a fact. Until you get things worked out, I want you to stay away from me."

"There's nothing to work out. I'll never forgive you, and I damn sure won't forget."

"How many times do I have to say it? I didn't *do* anything!"

Just as Santee uttered a particularly vulgar expletive, the front door opened.

Carol stood uncertainly in the front room, looking from Sloane's pale face and tumbled hair to Santee's livid glare and heaving chest. "Sloane, are you all right? Lucas, if you've hurt her . . . !"

Grateful for the interruption, Sloane was still embarrassed that anyone else should have become involved. "I'm all right, Carol. What are you doing here?"

"I got worried after Lucas called last night. Maybe I shouldn't have told him where you live, but I thought if you talked again . . . guess I was wrong."

"Don't worry, Carol," he sneered. "Your friend's neck and her virtue are both intact." He snatched his hat from the table and slammed the door, hard, on his way out.

Sloane stalked upstairs to her worktable and began pummeling a piece of clay, Carol close on her heels.

"Therapy?" Carol inquired cheekily.

"A few more encounters with that man, and I'll need intense psychoanalysis!" The clay slapped against the flat surface of the table with a satisfying splat.

Carol laughed, shaking her head. "This has got to be the strangest romance in history."

Incredulous, Sloane stared at the blonde. "That's the most ridiculous thing you've ever said! That crazy cowboy would strangle me if he could get away with it."

"That's not all he'd do. When I came in, you looked like a woman who'd just been thoroughly kissed, in spite of the daggers you were throwing at each other."

"One kiss does not a romance make, Carol."

"Oh, it's more than the kiss. It's in your eyes when you look at him, and in his, too. He just doesn't know it yet. But I think you do. You just don't want to admit it."

Sloane dropped her eyes, miserably aware of the truth in Carol's words. Her life had turned into one huge mess, and she hadn't the faintest glimmer of how to handle it.

By the time Lucas got back to Crooked Creek, he was in a rare mood, startling several of the men with his unprovoked temper and prompting Salty, the cook, to remark: "Gotta be a woman. Only thing I know can turn a good man into a lunatic."

"Probably that Taylor woman," Jimbo added. "He's been on a tear ever since she came out here that day."

Santee took the new stallion out for a hard run, hoping to exorcise his frustration. It helped some, but not much. Her words kept going around in his head: "I didn't *do* anything!" If he didn't know better, he'd swear she was telling the truth. But did he know better? Had he put the pieces together wrong?

He remembered her eyes flashing defiance at him, the way she'd thrust out her chin when he provoked her. But most of all, he could still taste her mouth. And it was good.

She dreamed again that night, but this time there were subtle differences. Michael's face, as he closed the door against her plea, altered slightly, his cheeks sliding into harder angles, brown hair shading into black, blue eyes into gray. Santee's face. Chapman, too, seemed larger, and his voice echoed, surrounding her. Her dream self saw him brandishing the knife, then saw him again to the right, and yet again to the left. There was no escape.

It was still warm enough in Dallas that the army surplus field jacket made him sweat as he stood outside the patio doors, waiting a safe interval before he entered. Then he took a small tool from his pocket and, in a surprisingly short time, slid the door open.

He remembered this room. For a while, here in this room, he had had her. Softly, slowly, noiselessly, he crept around a chair, a small flashlight cutting the darkness with a thin beam. He wasn't sure exactly what he was looking for, but he'd know when he found it.

He couldn't believe his luck. It lay on the desk in plain sight. A small page with a handwritten name and number. He slipped it into his shirt pocket and left the way he had come. He didn't bother closing the door; the lock was broken anyway.

Chapter Five

SLOANE STOOD BESIDE the shiny countertop and waited for the coffee to perk. A new week, she thought, glancing at the calendar on the kitchen wall. And only a month until the opening of her show. According to Carol, it would be a major event in Denver, quite possibly the vehicle that would launch her into a real career, with all the recognition and acclaim that any artist craves. She should be jittery with excitement; why was she so unaffected, almost numb?

Santee. Damn him. He had taken over her life, her thoughts, her dreams, and she bitterly resented her inability to break the hold. Even her work reflected the influence of his silent, unseen presence. The model of his head she had started Friday night was still on her worktable, despite her resolve to use it for target practice. She had even gone so far as to set it out on the sun deck, hoping the birds would use it for a perch, but within an hour it was back in the studio, perversely stealing her attention from other, more important projects.

She would have *one* cup of coffee, she vowed, then she would buckle down and do some serious work. The small, wood mountain lion was nearly finished, and she was eager to get started on some preliminary sketches for an idea she'd been considering for several weeks—a cowboy sitting on his heels beside a newborn calf, his hat pushed back on his head. As always when she was anticipating the start of a new piece, she felt pressured to finish the current one. Surely some good hard work would eliminate her preoccupation with the problem of Lucas Santee.

One cup became two, and still she sat at the dining table trying not to think of him and failing miserably. During the long night she had been over all the angles, examined every option. He was drawn to her, that much was obvious. But he didn't trust her, despite what she'd told him. Rena's ghost would always be there between them. And even if the obstacle were overcome, what good would it do? Special as he was, he was only human; and once he found out about her, realized she wasn't normal, he would despise her. So what was left? An affair? It wasn't out of the question. The physical attraction between them was strong enough to overcome the hostility on a temporary basis. But she knew herself; a brief fling with Santee would destroy her. If she couldn't have him forever, she didn't want him at all. And she couldn't have him forever.

The clock above the sink said nine-thirty. She had spent forty-five minutes doing absolutely nothing but brooding. By sheer force of will, she made it upstairs to the studio, where the little mountain lion looked at her reproachfully through half-carved eyes as though to say, *"Stop mooning around like an adolescent and come back to the real world."*

Unfortunately, this was the real world, at least her somewhat limited portion of it. She would have to deal with Santee, or rather her reaction to him, sooner or later. Maybe with a little concentration and hard work, it would be later. Sooner should be devoted to her work, her art, her future. She picked up a carving tool and began to sculpt.

Sometime later the shrill jangle of the telephone broke her concentration with a jolt that shocked her heart into a swift pounding. Usually she took the phone off the hook when she didn't want to be disturbed, but today she had forgotten.

She answered the bedroom extension. "Hello?" No one replied.

Her voice was still a bit breathless with surprise, so she spoke louder. "Hello? Is anyone there?"

Silence was the only response, a rather noisy silence filled with faint crackles of static and the hum of distance. It could be Michael, she realized, calling from Dallas; maybe there was a bad connection.

"Michael, is that you?"

She counted three, four, five more seconds of silence before the connection was broken. Had she really heard someone breathing, or was it only line interference?

Puzzled, she replaced the receiver, wondering if she should call him back. Maybe he had news of Chapman. No, she decided, if it was important, he'd call back in a few minutes. Most likely it was a wrong number. She turned back to the worktable and the patient mountain lion.

By three o'clock that afternoon, the lion was finished. It was really good, she thought, turning it in her hands so that she could appraise it from every angle. Maybe the best she'd ever done. Wood had always been her favorite medium, and she had had more practice on animals. Capturing the essence of personality in a human figure was infinitely more difficult. But her confidence was growing apace with her skill, and she could hardly wait to get started on the new piece.

As she set aside the lion, her eyes strayed to the bust of Santee, that traitorous piece of clay that tempted her to touch it, then mocked her when she did. She ran her fingers lightly across the forehead, then over the firm, sensual mouth and down to the dimple in the center of a strong, square jaw. Such strength was incongruous in soft clay; walnut would suit his character much better, hard and unyielding, beautiful yet apt to wound you with a splinter if you caressed it.

Once more the telephone interrupted her train of thought, but this time she was grateful for the distraction.

"Sloane? It's Michael." Even through the distortion of hundreds of miles, the urgency in his voice was sharp and clear. Her stomach knotted uncomfortably.

"Yes, Michael. What is it, what's wrong?"

"Someone broke into the house last night." He paused as though uncertain what to say next.

"Michael, just say it!"

"The only thing I found missing was the slip of paper with your phone number on it. Luckily, I had already written it in the address book. And, Sloane . . . Chapman's gone."

"Gone? You said he was working, that you had someone watching him!"

"He showed up for work this morning, but he left for lunch about eleven-thirty and didn't come back. The detective checked his rooming house; he wasn't there and it looks like he's moved out. His family hasn't heard from him for a week or so."

An ugly thought raised ripples of goose flesh along her arms.

"Michael, did you call me earlier, several hours ago?"

"No. I thought about it, but I wanted to be sure . . ."

"It was him! He called me! It was long distance, but nobody answered me. I thought it might have been you. I know it was him, checking out the phone number!''

"Sloane, listen to me! Calm down and think about it. I wanted you to know, just in case, but the chances of him finding you are one in a million. The house has been burglarized before; whoever it was could have been frightened away before he had a chance to take anything. And that note with your phone number could have been blown off the desk, thrown away, anything. The detective is still looking. Chapman will probably turn up in a bar somewhere.'' He paused for a moment, giving the words time to soak in. "Just take it easy and don't jump to conclusions. Maybe I shouldn't have called, but you said you wanted to know everything.''

She felt as uncertain as he sounded. Yes, she *did* want to know everything, to be prepared in case Chapman tried to carry through with his threats. But a series of coincidental circumstances could blow it all out of proportion, causing her to overreact and waste time in fearful anticipation of something that might never happen.

"Okay, Michael, I'm all right now," she said shakily. "I'm glad you called, and I'll try to be rational about it. What do you think I should do?''

As soon as the words were spoken, she knew what his answer would be.

"Come home. Let me take care of you.''

"I am home, Michael,'' she replied gently.

"All right, I won't press you," he said after a long moment. "I'll make a few calls, see what I can turn up. In the meantime, I think you should talk to the local authorities, alert them to the situation. In a small town like Snowcrest, a stranger will be spotted easily. Tell them they can request any information they need from the Dallas police. And why don't you stay somewhere else for a few days, just until we locate Chapman."

"You're right. I'll drive in this afternoon and see the sheriff. And I'll stay with a friend of mine in Denver, Carol McIntyre. She's in the telephone book if you need to call me there. You will call, no matter what you find out?"

"I promise. Try not to worry, it's probably nothing. I'll be in touch." His voice was sad, but somehow more caring, more—mature. She suspected Michael had done his own share of growing up in the past three years.

The first few tentative snowflakes were beginning to fall as she carefully maneuvered the Celica down the winding gravel road from the cabin to the main highway. By morning, she knew, the whole area would be blanketed in a fine, bright white powder. In a few weeks, winter would be settled in to stay, the snowfall wet and heavy, making driving more hazardous and less frequent. For now it was lovely, an experience to be savored, but within a few days even a simple trip to the grocery store would have to be planned carefully.

During the previous winters she had stocked the pantry against the probability of being snowbound, but this year, she thought, might be a good time to trade in the Celica for a heavier vehicle, something that would get her into town through the worst weather. Besides, she would feel so much more secure knowing she had safe transportation through muddy, icy roads, just in case . . .

If I'm that afraid, she chided herself, *why not go back to Dallas, back to Michael? He seems to have changed, to have a real concern for me now. Could I learn to care for him again? Would it be worth the effort to find out?*

With characteristic honesty, she answered herself without hesitation: *Santee's changed everything. If I hadn't met him, I would be more than tempted to go back to Michael and try again. But not now. Whatever happens—or doesn't happen— with Santee, I could never settle for second-best with Michael.* And she knew, with unshakable conviction, that second-best was all her ex-husband could ever be.

The sheriff's office was housed in a low solid-looking red brick building on the town square. Sloane had met him once, briefly, shortly after moving to Snowcrest; she remembered thinking at the time that he was one of those innately honest, competent men that people instinctively trust and respect, a born enforcer.

There were plenty of parking spaces around the square. During the winter months the population dwindled to a couple of hundred people, mostly old-timers and shopkeepers. The tourists who were hardy enough to brave the weather preferred to spend their money at Vail, and the more affluent citizens took up residence in California or Florida, trusting in Sheriff Will Lambert to dutifully protect their property while they were away acquiring winter tans.

Sloane was faintly amused at their attitude; apparently it hadn't taken her long to develop the old-timers' disdainful opinion of the giddy social set that sang the praises of this lovely country to anyone who would listen but were too fainthearted to stick around to see it when it was truly splendid.

She parked directly in front of the door with its stencilled label: "Sheriff's Office."

The air inside was warm and aromatic with the smell of pipe tobacco. A tall, barrel-chested man rose from his desk to greet her.

"It's a pleasure to see you, Miss Taylor. A social call, I hope?" His slightly pudgy face had an agelessness that belied the gray streaks in his sandy hair.

"I'm surprised you remember me, Sheriff," she said, seating herself in a chair next to his desk.

"Well, you created a little stir when you moved in. We don't get many pretty young artists up this way, at least not many who stick around."

"Should I apologize for causing a stir," she smiled, "or just take it as blatant flattery?"

"Definitely flattery, ma'am. Besides, we could

use a little stirring up, just to keep us on our toes." He leaned back in his chair. "Now what can I do for you?"

"Well, it's rather confused," she began. "I hope I can make you understand . . ."

"Something to do with your trouble in Dallas?"

She looked at him blankly, taken aback for a moment; then she laughed. "Under any other circumstances, I'd be offended that you pried into my past, but now . . . well, it'll save a lot of explaining."

"Any time someone like you shows up out of nowhere, buries herself in the woods, and seems content to stay there, it sort of occurs to me that maybe they're hiding something. And if it's something dangerous or illegal, it could involve me sooner or later. I'd rather be prepared than surprised."

He listened quietly as she went over the events of the past week or so—Michael's letter, her conversation with him, then his last disturbing news. "The only thing missing is a piece of paper with my name and phone number on it. And now Chapman is missing too. He walked out on his job, and no one knows where he is."

"Could be he just got tired of the job. Or maybe he met a woman, moved in with her. It's not unusual for a man like Chapman to just drop out of sight."

"I know that. But Chapman isn't predictable or rational. And besides, there was the phone call."

"He called you?" Lambert sat up straighter in his chair; this was beginning to interest him more and more. Maybe the lady wasn't just jumping at shadows.

"I don't know. I mean, I don't know if it was Chapman. I got a call about noon today; but when I answered, no one said anything. And it was a long-distance call—you know how the line sounds?" Lambert nodded, and she continued. "And that's what he did before. He called to make sure I was in the house, I guess, or to intimidate me."

"Before? You mean back in Dallas?"

"Yes. He would call when I was alone or late at night, sometimes several times in a day. And it was always the same, just—breathing." The memory was chilling. "I think I have reason to be afraid, Sheriff. I know there's nothing you can do, right now, I mean. But if you could watch for strangers in town, or—whatever. And Michael said to tell you that if you needed more information, the Dallas police would be glad to cooperate. He also has a private detective trying to trace Chapman. They should have some news in a couple of days."

"I assume you're smart enough not to stay out there in the cabin alone until you know for sure Chapman's not hot-footin' it to Colorado?"

She nodded. "I'll be staying with a friend for a few days." She gave him Carol's name and number.

He walked with her to the door. "I do understand, Miss Taylor, but I'm still inclined to believe that our friend'll turn up right there in Dallas. Try not to worry. We'll keep our eyes open here in town, and I'll have my deputy make regular runs out by your place, just to look things over.''

"Thank you. You and Michael are probably right; I'm just being paranoid. But I intend to do everything I can to protect myself, anyway.''

"You're a smart lady. Let me know what Mr. Fielding turns up at his end.''

She breathed more easily during the drive back home. Surely it would all prove to be a false alarm. But if it wasn't, it sure felt good to have Will Lambert on her side.

Carol was delighted, though puzzled, at the prospect of having Sloane as a house guest for a few days. She'd been trying to get her friend back to the city ever since she'd moved away, and now she thought she saw her chance.

"By the time I get through reminding you of what you're missing," she cooed over the phone, "you'll be dying to come back to civilization. I know this *divine* man . . .''

"Carol, this isn't a mating expedition, so knock it off. I'll be there in a couple of hours. And you'd better not meet me at the door with a man tucked under each arm!''

"I suppose it would be rather a waste of time, now that you've sampled the fabulous Lucas. How was he, by the way?''

Sloane could visualize her friend's avid expression and had to laugh. "You're impossible. I'll see you soon."

Sloane packed lightly and efficiently, taking only the most casual clothes: jeans, sweaters, flat shoes. Not only would the suitcase be lighter but Carol couldn't expect her to go partying in Levis.

Just as she tossed the last few articles in the pink cosmetic case, the phone rang. She answered it eagerly, hoping to hear Michael's calm, reassuring voice telling her Chapman had been found happily wallowing in a Dallas gutter.

But there was no reply to her hello, only cold and distant static. Shocked, she held the receiver to her ear until the dial tone clicked in. She was trembling as though deeply chilled, yet her palms were slippery with perspiration. Slamming the receiver back onto the hook, she snapped her cases together and flew down the stairs, pausing only to slip into a heavy coat.

As she struggled with large, clumsy buttons, the phone shrilled again.

Don't answer it, she commanded herself. *Just get in the car and leave!* But as the bell jangled repeatedly, she unwillingly picked it up; it might be Michael.

"Sloane? Are you there?" Carol's voice was so normal, so sane, Sloane was near tears with relief.

"I'm here, Carol. What is it?"

"Are you having trouble with your phone lines? I just tried to call and couldn't get through."

"It was you? I thought . . ."

"Sloane, talk louder, I can barely hear you."

"I'm leaving now, Carol. What is it?"

"I just remembered I have to go to dinner with a client, and I don't want to leave the door unlocked. The key will be in the planter by the neighbor's door, 3-G. Make yourself at home; I won't be late."

"Okay. Don't hurry, I'll be fine."

She hadn't thought to ask Carol if she'd tried to call earlier, around noon. Denver to Snowcrest was long distance, and if there were trouble on the line, it would explain all.

It was the most comforting thought she'd had in a long time.

He watched the telephone cord dangle, swinging back and forth gently. It reminded him of a noose, curling into a loop just about the size of *her* neck. Maybe he wouldn't use the knife this time.

The trace of panic in her voice had gratified him. He wanted her to be afraid. It was more fun that way.

Chapter Six

"EVENIN', LUCAS. WHAT brings you to town so late? I was just getting ready to close up shop. No trouble, I hope." Will Lambert stretched his bulk across the desk to shake Santee's hand, a smile of genuine pleasure lit up his ruddy face. "I don't get to see much of you anymore."

"It's good to see you, Will. No, no real trouble yet, but it could be brewing. I noticed some tire tracks a few weeks back, right after the last rain. They led back into the property to the old homestead cabin near the deadfall. And this morning, I spotted a pickup full of teenagers leaving by the back road."

"Recognize them?"

"No, but I got the license number." Santee

pulled a slip of paper from his coat pocket and handed it to the sheriff. "Thought maybe you could check it out for me."

Lambert nodded. "Sure thing. Our local boys might just be looking for a new place to spoon."

"Probably. But I like to know who's trespassing. Strangers poking around my stock make me a little edgy," he replied as he turned up his coat collar and moved toward the door. "I'd appreciate anything you can do, Will."

"Hold it, Lucas." Lambert gestured toward the chair next to his desk. "I'd like to talk to you about something if you've got a minute."

Santee frowned as he sat down. "What's wrong?"

"That's what I wanted to ask you." Opening a drawer, Lambert took out a pipe and began to tamp it down. "I've been hearing some talk around town, and I think there are a few things you oughta know."

"About what?" He didn't care much for the direction this conversation was taking.

"About Sloane Taylor. Jimbo heard you lettin' her have it about Rena. Says you had some pretty rough things to say, like it was her fault Rena was killed." The pipe was laid aside, forgotten, as Will searched his friend's face.

Santee glowered. "It was none of his concern, and it's none of yours either. Last I heard, it wasn't against the law to dislike somebody."

"Don't get your back up. Take it the way it's meant—friendly. I just hate to see Miss Taylor get the wrong end of a bad deal. I like her. She's got a lotta spunk.''

"We're talking about two different women then. The one I know sent Rena out to do a job she was afraid to do herself, because she knew she was in danger. She even gave Rena her coat to wear, told Rena to take her car. If you can see spunk in that, you've got damn funny notions.''

"Not funny notions, just more accurate information. All those stories in the Dallas papers weren't true, Lucas. It was her husband who sent Rena out that night after his wife refused to go. And she had told him why she didn't want to go out. So you're blaming the wrong person. And another thing,'' he cut in over Santee's protest, "if it weren't for Miss Taylor, that Chapman guy probably wouldn't have been caught in the first place.''

"What are you talking about?'' The bravado was fading fast. Had he made the most disastrous mistake of his life? "The police caught him. She had nothing to do with it.''

"Boy, you're way outta line on this. Nobody even knew who Chapman was, but they figured when he found out he'd got the wrong woman, he'd come back after the right one. That lady you've been abusing put her life on the line to help catch him, playing sitting duck to lure him in. And she damn near died because of it. It just might interest you to know that weirdo got past the police, into her house, and cut her throat before they pinned him down. That's the story that *wasn't* printed in the papers, and it's the real one."

Shocked into silence, Santee could do nothing but stare at his clenched fists. He remembered her saying, that day at the ranch, "Newspapers don't always report everything." Damn, why hadn't he listened? Was it too late to turn it all around?

Lambert continued, "Now you owe her, Santee. She's a fine lady, and she doesn't deserve what you've been dishin' out. Especially now. She needs all the friends she can get."

"What do you mean, 'especially now'?" Santee muttered, still fighting the sense of shame that engulfed him.

Lambert marvelled that a man as much in love as Lucas Santee could have caused himself so much misery. He dreaded telling his friend the rest, but it had to be said. "Chapman's loose. Legally loose. There's some reason to believe he's lookin' for Miss Taylor. He made his intentions pretty clear at the trial, and he's been reported prowling around her ex-husband's place in Dallas, probably lookin' for her."

Santee stiffened, a dangerous stillness altering his features. "How'd you find out?"

The implacable steel of his voice raised the hair on Lambert's neck; he'd hate like hell to be in Chapman's shoes if Lucas ever got hold of him. "She just left here, not more than half an hour ago. She's kinda spooked. Somebody broke into Fielding's house a couple of nights ago. Didn't take anything but a slip of paper—it had her phone number on it. And she got a peculiar call earlier today, seems to think it was him, tryin' to track her down.''

Santee jumped from the chair cursing. ''Why the hell didn't she tell me? Crazy woman!'' As soon as the words were spoken, he realized how asinine they sounded. He glared at Will in anticipation of what would undoubtedly be a telling remark. He wasn't disappointed.

''Way I hear it, you weren't doing a lot of listening, friend.'' Lambert grinned broadly. ''Maybe you oughta try again. She's staying in town with Carol McIntyre.''

''You don't have to tell me what kind of fool I've been,'' Santee growled. ''I've got that much figured out. Now what happens if Chapman shows up here in Snowcrest?''

''Nothing, unless he actually threatens her.'' Will frowned. ''Legally he's free to travel anywhere he wants. Until he breaks the law, I can't do anything but advise him to move on.''

''Well, I can do more than that,'' Santee vowed through clenched teeth, ''a lot more.'' The killer who murdered his sister was free. A woman who had come to mean a great deal to him had been attacked before and was once again in danger. *Maybe Chapman should come here*, he thought grimly. *Yes, he wanted him here. Then he would end it, once and for all*.

* * *

Carol's apartment was luxurious but small. The extra bedroom was barely large enough for a single bed, a night stand, and a dresser, but the view was magnificent. Through the darkness, tiny street lights twinkled along the curve of Canyon Road like miniature Christmas tree lights, while the snowflakes swirled gently in the luminous glow of the lights in the courtyard immediately below. Not one footprint marred the serenity of the soft whiteness that was already beginning to drift along the sides of buildings and curbs.

Sloane stood silently, lost in the pleasure of the winter scene, remembering how transported she had been that first winter in Colorado when she walked for hours through the first snowfall in the mountains. She didn't think she could bear it if she had to give up her haven to move back to the city. But if the problem with Chapman wasn't resolved soon, she would have to seriously consider doing just that. It would be impossible to live with the strain of isolation and uncertainty.

Finally, she let the curtain fall back into place and walked into the living room. Carol had thoughtfully laid wood in the small freestanding fireplace and had even left the makings for hot chocolate neatly arranged on the immaculate kitchen counter. Sloane put a match to the lighter pine before going back into the bedroom to change into a nightgown and robe. By the time she'd brushed her hair and made her nightly toilette, the logs were blazing cheerily. She had just finished stirring the chocolate when the door opened to admit Carol.

"Perfect timing," Sloane said. "The cocoa's just finished. How are the roads?"

"Not so bad as they're going to be in a couple of days. Actually, it's a glorious night. Remind me I said that when it's time to battle the slush to get to work tomorrow morning." Carol shook out her coat and scarf and hung them in the closet near the front door. "Now, are you going to tell me what's going on or do I have to worm it out of you?"

"There really isn't that much to it," Sloane replied, bringing two steaming mugs from the kitchen. Carol took hers and they both sank into the deeply cushioned sofa. "It's just a precaution. Michael called today. He thinks Chapman may be looking for me, so we decided to err on the side of prudence until we know for sure."

Carol's frown spoke clearly of her confusion. "What do you mean, he's looking for you? I heard he was caught, put on trial, and locked away in a mental institution."

"He was released about a month or so ago. But it's okay, Michael's having him watched and . . ."

"Do you mean to tell me there's a madman on the loose, looking to add your scalp to his collection, and you're sitting calmly sipping hot chocolate? Sloane, I don't believe this! Aren't you frightened? Why aren't you hiding in the closet? And you left the door unlocked!"

"For God's sake, Carol, the man was in Dallas at eleven-thirty this morning. I hardly think he's had time to track me down. Besides, it's probably all a false alarm. Michael has a private detective working on it. I expect to hear from him tomorrow or the day after, then I'll be out of your hair."

"Damn my hair! It's your life I'm worried about! Sloane, please, *please,* give up this back-to-nature kick and move back to Denver. You can stay here with me until you find a place of your own. It's not safe out there!"

Sloane laughed lightly, unwilling to hear anyone else put into words what she had so recently worried about herself. "It's not safe anywhere, Carol, certainly not here. I'll match Snowcrest's crime statistics against Denver's any day."

"Don't be reasonable, darling. This is the time for raw emotionalism. You need protection, a place to hide, a crowd to get lost in. Out there in hicksville, you shine like a beacon. You know I'm right!" Carol was like a terrier worrying a bone, determined to tear it apart even though the meat was long gone.

"If you're going to keep this up, I'll go to bed now," Sloane threatened. "I'm tired and upset, and I don't need your badgering."

"All right, don't get cranky. We'll talk about it tomorrow. Would you like to hear about my date?" She yawned and stretched sensuously.

"Not particularly," Sloane answered wryly. "Especially if you were entertaining Lester the Molester again.''

Both women laughed at the reference to one of the gallery's most difficult clients, old Mr. Lester, who fancied himself among the world's greatest connoisseurs of wine and women. Carol had regaled Sloane many times with hilarious stories of his attempts to rival Valentino in style and technique while Carol tried valiantly to sidestep his advances without losing his account.

"No, thank God. Old Lester's finally found himself a sweet young thing with dollar signs in her eyes. Tonight I lucked out. Van Buren's hired a new assistant, and I have the pleasure of acclimatizing him to Denver society. He is *such* a doll.''

At that moment a deep, reverberating gong interrupted the conversation. Sloane was startled when Carol answered the phone instead of the door, and even more surprised when she heard, "Yes, she's here. Just a moment." Carol covered the mouthpiece with her hand. "It's Lucas. He wants to talk to you.''

"No!" Sloane whispered frantically. "I don't want to talk to him tonight. Tell him I'm asleep."

Carol dutifully relayed the message, then extended the receiver. "He says you'll either talk to him on the phone or in person, but either way, it'll be tonight.''

Sloane bounded across the room and snatched

the offending instrument from Carol's hand. "What do you want?" she hissed.

"Why didn't you tell me Chapman was loose?" She could hear clearly the barely controlled anger in his voice. "And that he's out to kill you?"

"Because it's none of your business, Santee."

"You little fool! Everything about that creep is my business. He killed my sister, and that makes it my business! Now I want to talk to you. It seems there's quite a lot you haven't told me."

"Santee, my patience is wearing thin. I don't *want* to talk to you, and I'm not going to talk to you—not about Chapman, not about *anything*! How did you find out, anyway?"

"I thought you didn't want to talk about it," he replied maddeningly.

Sloane covered the mouthpiece and asked, "Carol, does he know where you live?"

"No, I don't think so."

"Good." And she slammed the receiver down, hard.

Carol raised a perfectly arched eyebrow mockingly. "That's telling him."

Sloane shot her a venomous look. "I'm going to bed. If he calls back, it's *your* problem."

Within minutes, she was angrily punching her pillow into shape, wondering how she would ever get to sleep with her brain racing around in circles. She listened intently, but the phone didn't ring again. Half an hour later, she heard Carol rustling around in the next bedroom. Soon afterward, the apartment was quiet and she drifted off to sleep, too worn out to keep up the effort of worrying.

Sloane was jolted awake when something plopped onto her midsection. Jerking upright, she saw a black felt Stetson, droplets of melted snow dampening her belly.

"I thought I wanted to wring your neck, but I've changed my mind," Santee drawled from his vantage point at the open door of her bedroom.

"You miserable sneak!" she raged, fully awake and ready for battle. "How did you get in here? How long will it take you to leave?"

"Quite a while, if I have anything to say about it." His eyes skimmed her, making her acutely aware of her state of undress. With a shriek, she threw a pillow in his face, then lunged for her robe. "Santee, you've got thirty seconds to get out of here before I . . ."

"Call the police? Try Will Lambert. He's expecting to hear from you anyway." His eyes crinkled at the corners as he laughed, obviously enjoying himself immensely.

"Lambert? *He* told you?" she sputtered, struggling into the suddenly unmanageable robe. "That was confidential information—he had no right . . . !"

"He's not your lawyer, your doctor, or your priest. But he is my old friend. Besides, he was worried about the way I've been treating you." In one long stride he was next to her, his warm hands grasping her shoulders gently. "Look, I'm sorry if

I startled you. But I meant it when I said we were going to talk. There's a lot I want to know, and I'm entitled to some answers.''

She twisted away from his touch; it was disturbing, even through her anger. ''I don't think you're entitled to anything. Will you please leave?''

''No, but I will plug in the coffee pot while you do whatever it is you do first thing in the morning. Carol left a note saying it was all set and ready to go.''

Sloane couldn't believe what she was hearing. ''Carol *knew* you were coming? She's already gone to work?'' She made a mental note to have a long and interesting talk with Carol.

''Yep. She called last night to tell me that if I came early, we'd have most of the day to work out our—problems.'' He looked as though he wanted to touch her again, and she didn't think she could bear it.

''Oh, that traitor! Just get out of my way!'' She brushed past him haughtily in a swish of satin and slammed the bathroom door behind her.

She lingered as long as possible, washing her face twice, brushing her teeth, arranging her hair. When she realized she was putting on makeup, she angrily scrubbed off the lipstick with a tissue. The man was making her crazy, and she was primping for him! She didn't need this, not now. Chapman was trying to kill her, and Santee was—what was he trying to do? What did he really want? Where was her bloody intuition when she needed it? Okay, she would give him the information he asked for, answer his questions, and maybe he'd go away. She devoutly hoped so. She simply didn't have the strength to keep him at arm's length, even had she wanted to; and she had a strong hunch it would come to that before the day was over. Where he was concerned, her pride made a mighty thin shield.

When she entered the living room, he was sprawled in one corner of the sofa, coffee in hand. "Yours is there, on the coffee table."

She took the cup, seating herself in a chair as far away as she could get. "What did Lambert tell you? And why?"

"I told you, he was defending you. And he told me a lot I should have known before. I was wrong about you, Sloane. I apologize." His eyes were as soft as his voice. "Why didn't you tell me about Chapman?"

"You already knew about Chapman." She knew what he really meant but was perversely determined to make him drag it out of her; why make it easy on him? He certainly hadn't cut her any slack.

His abrupt anger startled her. "Damn it, Sloane, don't play these games with me! Now give me some answers! Why did he come after you in the first place?"

"All right!" She could tell he was at his limit, but then, so was she; if only he would go away . . . "Chapman was released, he's back in Dallas, and there's a chance he's looking for me. Is that all, Mr. Santee?''

"No, it's not all," he growled. "Why is he looking for you?"

At a loss for words, Sloane could only stare at him indignantly. He settled back against the sofa, looking smug.

"You weren't going to tell me, were you? About being the sacrificial goat in their little trap, about getting your throat cut while your lily-livered ex-husband was out sticking his head in the sand?"

She hadn't believed she could get any angrier, but now she gritted her teeth to control the rage that welled up inside. "You're really unbelievable! First, you wouldn't listen to anything I had to say. Now you want to pick through every little detail. Has it ever occurred to you that some things might be too painful, too private to discuss?"

He came to kneel beside her and took her hand. "Yes, it has occurred to me. But I have a need to know, Sloane. I've been through some pain of my own, and I never even had the comfort of knowing why it happened. Now will you please talk about it?"

"All right," she capitulated. "But sit down first."

"Why? Do I make you nervous?" he teased.

She shot him a hostile look but didn't answer. He was absolutely right. Just the touch of his hand made her heart stop.

"Okay, I'm safely sitting. Now talk."

She told him much the same thing she'd told Carol two days earlier, but he was after more.

"Seems farfetched that he'd resort to murder just because he was fired," he commented when she finished speaking.

"According to the psychiatrists who examined him, he has a pathological hatred of women. They think he's probably responsible for a couple of unsolved murders during the past ten years or so. He had a police record for assault and a history of mental instability. He was on probation when he worked at the house. Anyway, in his mind, I was to blame when he got fired and couldn't find another job. Then when he saw Michael and me on television during the campaign, it started to fester and grow, and he decided I had to pay for what I'd done to him."

"And then you helped nail him, making him more determined than ever. He won't give up, Sloane. As long as he's alive, you're not safe."

Shivering with reaction, she drew her feet up into the chair and hugged her knees. "I know. But I can't just keep running away. It has to end sometime. Michael's keeping him in sight, so maybe . . ."

"Michael!" Santee derided. "A fat lot of help he's been! I can't figure out why you ever married him."

His criticism of Michael was justified, she knew, but nevertheless she bristled. "You're awfully good at passing judgment, aren't you, Santee? First me, now Michael."

Silence stretched between them as conflicting emotions battled inside him. Semigraceful shame won. "I deserved that, I guess. I was a first-rate ass for not listening when you tried to explain, and God knows how much I regret the pain I caused you. But damn it all, this is different. He was your husband, Sloane, but he deliberately tried to sacrifice you to save his so-called career. Now you say he's trying to help you. How can you defend him?"

"Please, let's just stop this now," she interrupted. "Michael's the only help I've got, and he deserves credit for trying. Besides, I just don't want to discuss him with you. If you can't understand, I'm sorry, but that's the way it is." She didn't understand it herself. His mere presence in the room played havoc with her senses, upset her balance, took away her reason. The tightrope she constantly walked between trusting her instinct and trusting her reason became more frayed every time they were together, and she was dangerously close to falling. But she couldn't tell him that. "I know this seems to be my standard reaction to you, but would you go now? I really don't want to fight."

"No."

She sighed. "Why not? I *did* ask you nicely."

"Because I'm not through talking. Now tell me why you went to see Will yesterday."

"Didn't he tell you?"

"Yes, but I want to hear it from you. And this time, I'm listening to every word."

She didn't want to meet his eyes; if his face were as soft and caring as his voice, she'd break down. She looked at the coffee cup between her hands. "Michael said Chapman left his job yesterday around noon and didn't come back; then I got this funny call."

"You think it was Chapman?"

She shrugged. "I don't know who it was, but it scared me. I could tell it was long distance, but no one said anything. I didn't really put the pieces together until Michael called, then I went to see Lambert."

"And he advised you to stay with Carol for a while."

"Until Chapman's found. He and Michael both seem to think he'll turn up in Dallas."

"But you don't agree?" He watched her intently, alert for any indication she knew more than she was telling.

"I just don't know." Nervously, she brushed an errant lock of hair behind her shoulder. "Unless he's really well, unless he's a different person than he was three years ago—that Chapman wouldn't have given up. He was determined I should die. That Chapman would be on his way to Colorado right now."

The very lack of emotion in her voice chilled him. What terrifying memories did she have to live with? He couldn't even begin to comprehend all she had been through. And added to that burden was what he himself had done to her. That guilty knowledge made him ill. And determined.

"He hasn't paid for what he did. Not yet." His tone was calm, in contradiction to the dangerous implication.

She shifted uneasily. "That's not up to either one of us, Santee. I just want him to stay in Texas and away from me." She rose from the sofa, drawing her arms tightly around her. He made her feel so vulnerable, so exposed . . .

"Sloane, sit down," he said wearily, correctly interpreting her actions as a prelude to fight. "We'll never get anywhere with this relationship if you keep running away. Can't we just talk?"

"Relationship?" she questioned. "Are you conceding there is one?"

"Yes. I guess I am."

"All right," she agreed. "But can we discuss something besides Chapman? So far, we don't seem to have any other common ground."

He smiled. "We'll find something. Tell me about yourself. When did you get into sculpting?"

"Oh, I guess I've always been into it, but not seriously until I moved to Colorado. I took my degree in art history, thinking I'd go for my master's and eventually into teaching, but then I met Michael."

"And he didn't approve?" There was a wealth of meaning in his tone; apparently his opinion of Michael was rapidly being reinforced.

"Oh, I worked after we were married." She

neatly skirted the issue. "Campaigning, fund-raising, volunteer work. He ran for district attorney not long after we were married, so I got an early initiation."

"No children? Or didn't they fit into his plans?"

The remark threw an icy pall on the optimism that had, up to this point, been steadily growing, bringing back a flood of unpleasant memories, and suddenly she didn't feel up to coping with his questions. "Look, why don't we drop this? I can't believe the story of my marriage holds any real interest for you, so let's change the subject, okay?" Uncomfortably aware of how her seemingly abrupt mood swings might affect him, she stared at the floor, wishing she could explain.

He swore under his breath. "You are the most exasperating female! I'm trying to apologize. We got off to a bad start, mostly my fault, but when I try to turn things around, you cut me off."

"You're prying into my private life."

He drew a deep breath. "I get the point. No personal questions. Okay, how about neutral ground? My foreman's back on his feet, and the ranch can get along without me for a few hours. Let's do something, go out to breakfast maybe. Have you ever been to the Short Stack?"

"Once, a couple of years ago, and I loved it. It'll only take me a minute to get ready."

It didn't take her long to slip on her prettiest heavy sweater and to fluff her hair out over her shoulders. A quick glance in the mirror confirmed what she already suspected; she was virtually glowing with excitement, her cheeks flushed and brown eyes sparkling. And only a few minutes ago, she'd been yelling at him. Where Santee was concerned, she couldn't seem to strike a happy medium. At the moment, the prospect of breakfast with him seemed the brightest spot in a very long, very dark week.

She finished up with mukluks, a ski jacket, and a knit cap, then bounced into the front room.

Santee's appraisal made her more nervous than ever, but he seemed to like what he saw. That engaging smile she so loved spread from his mouth to his eyes, and he whistled appreciatively. "You look like an ad for a ski resort. The all-American beauty ready to hit the slopes of Vail."

He held the door for her. As she passed him, he slid his hand down the length of her hair, stopping at her waist. For just an instant their eyes met and held, an unspoken message flowing between them, fueled by the spark that leapt from his flesh to hers.

"Lady, I think we've got a problem," he said lightly, but the strain was evident in his voice. "We never know whether to kiss or kill."

His fingers were dancing a tingling ballet on the nape of her neck, and he was standing entirely too near. She couldn't speak.

"Sure you want to go out to breakfast?" he murmured close to her ear, his breath stirring her hair.

132

"No," she answered softly, "but I think we'd better."

He hadn't exaggerated the quality of the food in the small restaurant. They had been served stacks of the best pancakes and sausage Sloane had ever tasted, complemented by whipped homemade butter, thick blueberry syrup and steaming black coffee.

"What a feast!" she said, pushing her plate away. "Many more like this and I'll look like a dumpling."

"Nothing wrong with that," he smiled. "My father used to say there was nothing better than an ample woman on a cold night."

"Tell me about your folks, Santee. Your dad started the ranch, didn't he?"

"Yeah, he came here from Kansas during the depression. He worked at just about anything and everything, saving every penny until he could buy the original fifty acres." He chuckled. "He was a real character, my old man. Always joking and laughing, and he worked harder than anyone I've ever known. I still miss him."

"And your mother?" She could hardly believe the intimacy of the mood they were sharing and she reveled in it.

"My mother." He closed his eyes for a moment, his face softening. "She was incredibly gentle and loving, but tough as nails underneath it all. Dawn to dusk, she worked right by Dad's side, building fences, raising barns, breaking horses.

She used to tell about tying me in a sling and carrying me on her back all day while she and Dad worked. She said that until I learned to walk, that was the only way I could sleep."

"Margaret's told me a little about her. She sounds like a very special lady," Sloane said softly.

He nodded. "One in a million. She had a lot to contend with in the early years, but I never once saw her angry or vindictive or defeated. Once, I remember, I came home with a bloody nose from a fight. I must've been about eight or nine. Somebody at school called her a dirty Indian and said my dad was a 'squaw man.' I didn't know exactly what a 'squaw man' was, but I could tell it wasn't a compliment. Well, Mother washed my face, never saying a word. Then she told me I better get used to it if I expected to wipe out ignorance and prejudice with my fists, and she asked if I wanted her to fix up a first-aid kit to take to school." He laughed at the memory. "Yeah, she was something else. But I guess you feel that way about your mother, too—that there's no one else in the world quite like her."

"I don't remember much about her," she hedged. The lie came easily; after all, she'd had years of practice. "She died when I was nine; she'd been ill for several years before, and I had to stay with relatives most of the time." That much at least was the truth.

"What about your father? Brothers and sisters?"

"No, there was just me and Mother." She

couldn't stand what she saw in his eyes—tenderness, sympathy . . . pity? "How about some more coffee?"

By the time they left the Short Stack, another inch of snow had accumulated and the wind had picked up, blowing a thin white veil across the windshield that was as effective as a blanket in obscuring visibility. Santee edged the pickup along slowly. The flap of the wipers punctuated the silence inside the cab. Santee was engrossed in maneuvering the truck through the slushy streets, while Sloane was far away in another time.

His shared memories had resurrected her own childhood more painfully than anything had done in years. He had asked about her past with genuine interest, and she was ashamed of her evasiveness. But there was just no way she could share the anguish and fear of that long ago time.

After her mother's death, things had slowly improved. A succession of foster homes had made her miserable at first; but as she grew, she toughened, learning to hide her peculiar ability, and life became a bit more tolerable. Then, in her early teens, the Fosters had taken her in, and she gave thanks daily for that minor miracle. They were an older couple who, after having raised several children of their own, decided to share their warmth and love with the unwanted, rootless youngsters of Dallas. They taught her to reach as far as she could and keep stretching; they showed her she could be whatever she wanted, if she was willing to work for it. Mrs. Foster had died during Sloane's first year of college, and the old man followed soon after. But Sloane never let herself forget their gift of love and was deeply grateful to have known them, for they had been the closest thing to a family she'd ever known.

But those few happy years didn't erase the emptiness and terror of her early childhood nor dim the reality of her alienation from the rest of the world. No, she wasn't ready to share that with Santee.

. . . look like a kid with those apple cheeks and that silly Bullwinkle hat, she heard Lucas beside her.

"There's nothing at all silly about my hat," she retorted, grateful to be called back from her dark thoughts. "I think Bullwinkle is quite distinguished in a moosey sort of way."

His head snapped around, his face a mask of shocked surprise, as she continued. "Besides, there's still some kid left in all of us, don't you think? Who's your favorite cartoon character?"

"Snoopy, I guess," he replied warily, quickly recovering his composure. Sloane's face was untroubled and guileless. He was willing to lay odds she wasn't even aware of what had just happened; he wasn't absolutely sure of the facts himself. But unless he had been hallucinating, the lady had just done a pretty good imitation of reading his mind.

"Hey, what's wrong with you? Ashamed that

you got caught reading the funnies?'' An irresistible smile lit up her face, prompting him to grin in return.

"Remind me to show you my private cartoon collection sometime.''

"Aha! A variation on 'let me show you my etchings.' At least you're original. And I have to admit, I'm a sucker for L'il Abner.''

The teasing banter continued until they reached the apartment building. Sloane was out of the truck first, waiting for Santee to lock it up.

As he rounded the front fender, a wet snowball hit his chest, exploding into his face. "Gotcha!'' Sloane shouted, standing prudently behind a waist-high shrub.

"I guess that means it's my turn!'' He scooped up a handful of the icy stuff and threw it as he ran. His long legs gave him the advantage, and he caught her easily, picking her up and tossing her over one shoulder.

"That's not fair! You're bigger. And meaner! What are you doing?''

"Giving you your just desserts.''

The snow had drifted several feet high and a yard wide along the side wall of the building. While she kicked and slapped at his rear, Santee sized up the drift, made his calculations, then effortlessly lifted her in both arms and heaved.

Laughing and gasping with surprise, she lay for several seconds, half-covered with snow, her hair and face dripping. "I can't believe you did that! And I let you get away with it!"

He helped her to her feet. "Well, what can you do when you're outclassed? Admit it, you just weren't equal to the situation."

She read his thoughts and blushed, pulling her hands away. "I'd better get out of these clothes before they get stiff," she said, ignoring his last comment. "Thanks for breakfast."

"The least I can do is see you safely dry," he interrupted, taking her elbow in a firm grasp. "Besides, I could use another cup of hot coffee to fortify me for the trip home."

The apartment was warm and welcoming. She began to peel off the wet coat on her way to the bedroom. "I've got to take a hot shower. Why don't you reheat the coffee, and I'll be out in a second." She didn't wait for his reply nor even glance at him again in her haste to take her disturbing awareness of him into another, safer room.

True to her word, she didn't linger. After a few minutes of steaming water and a harsh lecture from her inner voice, she felt ready to face him again, confident that the visit could be concluded on a friendly but impersonal note. Not that that was what she wanted, but she knew it would be best in the long run. Back in the tiny bedroom, she unfolded jeans and a flannel shirt, then chose a pair of fuzzy booties instead of shoes.

"Hey, Santee," she called, not bothering to

turn toward the door, "would you mind starting a fire? I'm still cold . . ."

"No need to shout."

She whirled around, clutching the front of her robe tightly. He lounged in the doorway, watching her with disturbing intensity. Her heart pounded, and she was sure he could see the telltale throb through the smooth, thin fabric clinging to her still damp body.

She raised one hand nervously to tuck in an errant strand of hair that had escaped from the towel she wore turban-style around her head. "I'm still a little chilled." Why was her voice only a whisper, and why couldn't she stop staring at his chest, at the curling hair that peeked above the vee of his shirt?

He walked toward her, in slow motion it seemed, until he stood so close she could smell the faint musky scent of his aftershave. The pulse in his neck beat in time to her own, and she traced it with her eyes until it disappeared behind his ear into the thick tousled hair that looked as though he had repeatedly combed his fingers through it. Her knees went suddenly weak; a rush of heat swept over her. She took one backward step before her back touched the closet door.

"Do you know I dreamed about you last night?" he said huskily. "You looked just like this . . ."

"I don't want to hear."

He ignored her words, reaching out a large, sun-bronzed hand to tug the towel from her head.

When her hair lay tumbled about her shoulders, he touched it gently, twisting the strands around his long fingers.

"I remember how you feel, how you taste. I want you, Sloane."

She remembered too.

When he pulled her into his arms, a sweet tingle ran along the length of her body where he pressed against her. She lifted her face to meet his kiss, a deep, searing caress that excited her beyond belief. How could a mouth that hard and unyielding be so sweetly tender, coaxing feelings and desires from her that she had never known existed? How could his body, which she had never known, be so familiar, feel so right? And how could she surrender the deepest part of herself to a man who could never be a permanent part of her life?

But if she was surrendering, so was he, she suddenly realized; and it was such sweet sharing. Once again his touch had triggered the erratic psi and she knew his thoughts. His desire consumed him, yes, but there was more, much more. He was holding back, afraid to rush her response, afraid of losing her. He wanted everything she could give and to give her everything she had never known. He wanted to brand her with joy and pleasure, binding her to him forever. All this she knew in an instant, and the knowledge was glorious.

She ran her hands over his shoulders, down his torso. He was tanned down to the line of his low-fitting jeans; an image of his tall, perfect body, shirtless under the summer sun, glistening and warm as he threw his head back in laughter, filled her senses. It was a fantasy, indescribably lovely, yet so very real—or was it a glimpse of the future? The thought was immensely comforting.

Passion folded them in her mists, blessing them with that most precious of all her gifts—complete oneness.

"My beautiful girl," he whispered as he lifted her and strode to the bed.

She lay quietly in his arms, savoring the afterglow of the most incredible experience she had ever known. *Those romances hadn't lied after all*, she thought, giggling softly.

"Funny is *not* the way I would describe it," he said against her ear, kissing her neck. Just the sound of his voice was arousing.

"I was just remembering all those torrid romances I used to read when I was a kid. You know the kind—'throbbing desire' and all that. I used to think they were fairy tales, made up to keep foolish young girls like me believing Prince Charming really existed. Now I know—they were right."

He looked at her wonderingly. "Do you mean this is the first time you ever . . ."

She laid a finger against his lips. "Hush. No technical terms, please." She kissed him slowly, moving her lips against his while her fingers curled through his hair.

141

He pulled away a fraction of an inch and smiled into her eyes. "I never did light that fire."

"Oh yes you did," she whispered.

Much later, they lay dozing, idly touching, occasionally whispering, teasing. Sloane had never felt so at peace, so in tune with the universe. She had been well and truly loved, and now she glowed with contentment. She traced his lips, recalling with awe the perfection of their coming together, unwilling to break the enchantment. But the quality of the outside light had changed, becoming darker; it was late afternoon.

"Do you think we should get up?" she said reluctantly, sighing.

"Why? Tired of me already?"

"Just tired, period. Actually, I was thinking of Carol. She lives here, you know. She'll be home sooner or later."

He grimaced. "With her sense of timing, it'll probably be sooner."

She laughed and propped her head on her hand, leaning over to kiss his shoulder playfully. As he reached for her, the quietness was broken by the sound of a loud, deep gong.

"What the hell is that?"

"Carol's version of a ringing telephone. I don't want to answer it, but I'd better, just to shut it up." His eyes followed her as she left the room, lingering on the dimple at the base of her spine. Grudgingly he pulled on his jeans and shirt, and was sitting on the edge of the bed putting on his boots when she waltzed back into the room, her face beaming.

"Good news, I presume," he teased. "From your expression, I'd say you just won the sweepstakes."

"Better than that!" she exclaimed. "That was Michael. Chapman's still in Dallas. He just took the afternoon off to move. The detective found his new place and everything's okay. Isn't that great?"

Instead of answering, he looked away, finished putting on his boots. Sloane felt a prickle of unpleasantness, his thoughts seeping into her mind, and she cut off the reception abruptly. She didn't want to know for sure; the suspicion was bad enough.

"I thought you'd be pleased, happy for me," she said slowly. "But you're not, are you?" After what had gone before, it was like a slap in the face, knotting her stomach with coldness. His earlier words echoed in her mind: *He hasn't paid—not yet.*

He stood and reached for her. "Sloane, it's not that. I *am* glad . . ."

"No, you're not," she whispered. "You're disappointed! You want him to come here, even knowing it could cost my life." Her palm itched, she wanted so badly to slap him. "That's what you meant before. You'd rather see me in danger, just for the chance of getting him yourself." Tears of outrage slid down her cheeks. "I can't handle this, Santee. Please leave."

"Sloane, I can protect you, keep you safe. Listen to me . . ." But he couldn't quite find the words she needed to hear.

"Get out of here! Don't come back, don't call, just get out of my life!"

He tried to smile, a crooked twist of his mouth. "It's hard to take you seriously when you're naked."

"Oh, I'm serious, Santee. I utterly hate and detest you! And you'll never get another chance to hurt me." She ran into the bathroom, slamming the door so violently the little apartment reverberated with the sound.

He wanted to hold her, to explain, but still the words wouldn't come. Her pain hurt him more than his own, but he didn't know how to comfort her. Besides, he was afraid she was right. He finally picked up his hat and coat and left, closing the door quietly behind him.

Carol came home wearing an expectant air, peering closely into her friend's face hoping to find some trace that at last all was right with Sloane's world. "So how did things go today with Lucas?"

Sloane's expression was shuttered. She answered coldly, "I don't know what you mean."

Carol couldn't accept that; she was willing to bet her last cent that the National Guard couldn't have kept Lucas Santee away from that apartment. "You're lying, Sloane. Now what happened?"

"Drop it, Carol," Sloane warned.

For one of the few times in her life, Carol practiced tact and discretion. "Okay by me. What's for supper?"

Sloane shrugged. "I hadn't really thought about it. We can throw together a salad. I'm not very hungry."

"Sounds good. And I've got a bottle of wine that'll go great with a fire later."

Dinner was a silent affair for the most part. Carol talked about her day at the gallery, trying to amuse Sloane with anecdotes about the new assistant's first day on the job, but her replies were absentminded and disinterested.

Later they sat together sipping wine, Sloane watching the fire with a lost, little-girl expression that tore at Carol's heart. *Santee must really have outdone himself this time,* she thought angrily, wondering how two people who so obviously belonged together could create so much unhappiness for themselves. She refilled Sloane's glass. "Here, darling, drink up before the chill is gone. It's good for what ails you."

Sloane hardly seemed to notice as she drained the glass, her second one, nor did she divine Carol's intention in keeping the glasses filled as quickly as they were emptied. Soon the bottle was finished. Carol opened another, feeling sure Sloane would neither notice nor care that this time the wine was red instead of white.

By ten o'clock, Sloane was slumped dejectedly against the soft cushions, all her defenses shattered. "He did come today, Carol," she murmured. "You shouldn't have done it, you know. Set me up like that." She shifted to lay her head on Carol's lap, still talking, pouring out the story until she slipped into sleep. Being careful not to wake her, Carol draped a thick afghan over her friend.

"Damn that Santee," she muttered as she climbed into bed. "I'd shoot him myself if Sloane didn't have first refusal."

Chapter Seven

WHEN CAROL STUMBLED into the kitchen early the next morning, smells of freshly perked coffee and bacon tantalized her into awaking. Sloane was just buttering the toast and turned with a smile when she heard Carol's pleased exclamation.

"I thought I heard your alarm. Hope you're a breakfast buff; there's far too much here for just me."

"Not usually," Carol replied, stifling a yawn. "But that's because I'm too lazy to fix it. If you're applying for the job, you've got it."

Sloane set the bacon, toast, and coffee on the diminutive table, where place settings were already laid, complete with orange juice.

"Sloane, this is heaven! How did you manage,

after last night? I thought you'd sleep at least until noon.''

''Carol, about last night—'' Sloane began uncertainly, ''did I say anything? I mean, did I make a complete fool of myself?''

Carol's answer was somewhat muffled by a mouthful of food, but it was clear enough. ''You most certainly did say something, and it did you a world of good. You should loosen up like that more often, sweetie; it prevents ulcers and wrinkles.''

''And promotes hangovers.'' Sloane winced at the somewhat fuzzy memory of a predawn trip to the bathroom; she was thankful her recollection was a bit vague. ''What were you plying me with, anyway?''

''Plying?'' Carol laughed in genuine amusement. ''Dear one, you needed no coaxing. After the first glass, you were belting them back like a sailor on shore leave.'' She paused long enough to toss down a glass of juice in demonstration. ''By my estimate, you put away nearly two liters of vino all by your little lonesome. I had no idea you were such a heavy drinker!''

''Neither did I. Seriously, Carol, I'm very grateful for your friendship—and your tact. Whatever I said last night, thank you for listening and for caring.''

''My pleasure. I love having you here. You're like a sister. I've never had many close, *really* close friendships—at least not with women,'' she added impishly.

Carol's irrepressible good humor never failed to give Sloane a lift. Her friend seemed able to take all of life's vagaries with a grain of salt and a belly laugh; Sloane wished she could be more like that, instead of letting the hard knocks come out on top.

"I've enjoyed being here, too. I appreciate your letting me stay. Did I tell you I'm going back home today?"

Carol shook her head, her blue eyes serious and worried. "Not in so many words, but I expected it. Sloane, are you sure it's safe?"

"As sure as I can be. Don't worry, I won't take any chances. Actually, I think it was just a false alarm. Do you think I'd leave here if I didn't think it was safe?"

Carol wasn't convinced, but she knew it was useless to argue. "Just take care of yourself, okay?" she replied. "Besides being my best friend, I have a vested interest in your continued good health. Van Buren wants to meet with you Monday afternoon, and if you don't show up he'll fire me!"

"Oh, I'll make it. You know, I just realized yesterday how close the exhibition is. But I'm in pretty good shape, only a couple of pieces to finish up."

"Good. Van Buren was really impressed, Sloane. He seems to have a lot of plans for you."

If she didn't have the distraction of her upcoming opening to keep her on an even keel, Sloane thought, she'd be tempted to hide like a hermit from her pain and confusion. As it was, she might find the strength to get over Santee . . . if she could only stop thinking of him.

It was still early afternoon when Sloane arrived home. The simple, clean lines of the cabin were outlined with a layer of white, giving it an even more pronounced air of cozy solitude than usual as it nestled in the surrounding snow-brushed trees. Though the snow had stopped falling sometime during the previous night and the sun's brief appearance had cleared the streets and highways, the shelter of the deep forest had preserved the crystalline beauty of the cabin's snowy setting. The western sunlight danced off the snow-shrouded trees, skipped lightly off the cabin's front windows, then sprang away to play tag with the enfolding hills and more distant peaks.

Winter never failed to touch Sloane more deeply than any other season. The familiar shapes of trees and boulders were encased in an icy cocoon, waiting for spring's chisel to expose their hidden grace and symmetry once more. As she walked to the front door, she paused to look back at her footprints and felt a twinge of regret that nature's handiwork seemed always to be marred in some way by man's intrusion.

Once inside she could barely wait to unpack and settle into the comfortable familiarity of home. She wondered if everyone felt as she did about their houses, that there was a kind of welcoming and acceptance in the very structure, a special magic that glowed only for her. Sometimes she felt a bit foolish about her fierce possession. It was, after all, only a structure, built by someone she had never known. But she was willing to bet that very few people had ever felt the beautiful sense of *belonging* she experienced every time she walked through her door. *No,* she decided, *other people may love their homes, take pride in them, but only someone who spent her life on the outside looking in could feel what I do, the glory of being "in" at last, in a special place that's mine alone.*

With the approach of evening, it began to snow again, big, soft, plump flakes that promised hazardous road conditions for tomorrow's commuters. She leaned her forehead against the window frame and watched the flakes gently swirling in the glow of the security light that flickered on when dusk fell. Later in the year, when forage became scarcer, the deer would venture into that circle of light; last winter she had seen a beauty that eventually metamorphosed into an enchanting statuette, which turned out to be a minor masterpiece. *Yes, this is all I'll ever want,* she told herself. *Security, peace, a place to belong.*

But as she gazed through the windowpane, another face seemed to shimmer near her own reflection, a dark brooding face with piercing eyes and a firm mouth that could melt her with tenderness. And a little gremlin voice inside her whispered, *Liar. After Santee, you can never settle for being alone again.*

All in all, the next few days were relatively calm. The new figure was shaping up well, better than she had dared hope when she made the preliminary sketches. If the cowboy who knelt beside the calf bore an uncanny resemblance to Lucas Santee—well, she didn't think anyone else would notice. She felt she had captured the graceful ease of the lean cowboy, and the little animal on the ground beside him was as lifelike as she could have wished. Another day or so would see the carving completed.

Perched at her worktable, watching every move, stood the head she had never been able to put away completely, although she had at last conquered the urge to refine and finish it. *It would serve him right if I left him that way forever—half finished—the way I feel.*

Seemingly on cue, the phone rang. She knew who it would be before she lifted the receiver. She was right. Santee's deep drawl was demanding when she answered.

"I want to talk to you, Sloane."

"We've played this scene before," she replied, trying to put as much chill as possible into her tone. "I don't think there's anything new to add."

There was no mistaking his angry frustration. "Then explanations are only important when *you're* making them, is that it?"

She bit back the words she longed to say: *Please, please come to me, hold me, love me.* But the wound was too fresh and the gamble too great.

After all, he had never said he loved her. If he would only say those words. "Tell me truthfully you don't want to use me as bait to draw Chapman into your hands the way the police did three years ago. Make me believe you weren't just using me the day we made love. Convince me my safety is more important to you than getting even with Chapman. Tell me you love me." There, it was out. "Then I'll listen to you."

Later she was to wonder if she had been fair, if she allowed him enough time to answer. It wasn't, after all, a simple request. But at the moment, his silence seemed to stretch out forever, and she knew only that her plea had gone unanswered.

"I guess that's answer enough."

His voice reached her as she replaced the receiver. "Sloane, wait, you don't . . ."

This time she refused to cry, though her eyes burned and her throat ached with the effort. "No more tears for me," she whispered into the silence of the room. "I'll be damned if he'll ever make me cry again."

Sunday dawned bright and clear, the sky uncluttered by clouds for the first time in nearly a week. Although it was still very cold—about thirty-five degrees according to the radio—Sloane couldn't resist the opportunity to take one of her rambling walks. She hadn't been outdoors since before her trip to Carol's, and her body was rebelling against the confinement and lack of exercise.

In her eagerness to be out in the open, she didn't take time for breakfast, but pulled on an old pair of button-up Levis and a red turtleneck sweater. Then she did a slow pirouette in front of the full-length mirror that hung on the closet door and winced at what she saw.

It had been a while since she really paid attention to her looks, she realized now, and she was appalled at the amount of weight she'd lost. Even through the heavy clothes, she was noticeably thinner. Her hipbones jutted through the denim material of the jeans, and her fingers and wrists looked almost bony. She leaned closer and inspected her face. The hollows of her cheeks were deeper, and her brown eyes, already large, seemed enormous.

Well, that settles that, she told herself. No more skipping breakfast until I've gained ten pounds.

The eggs were whipped up, yellow and frothy in the bowl, and she was grating cheese for an omelet when the sound of a car pulling up outside arrested her attention. She glanced at the clock—it was only eight-thirty. The only person she knew who might be up and out at this early hour on a weekend was Santee. But surely he wouldn't be coming here, she thought wildly, not after that last phone call. Instead of the peremptory knock on the door which she half-expected, there came instead a delicate rapping, followed by Carol's piping voice. "Up and at 'em, lady. It's *cold* out here!"

"Why didn't you use your key?" scolded Sloane,

admitting her shivering friend to the warmth of the living room.

Carol turned reproachful blue eyes on her. "Are you kidding? After what happened last time, barging in on you and Lucas? I'd rather freeze." She shrugged out of her full-length fur coat while Sloane stared in amazement.

"I'm surprised you didn't, in *that* costume!" She shook her head, bemused by Carol's outrageous appearance—a black sequined pantsuit with a halter top, the legs gathered at the ankle, and spaghetti-strap sandals with stiletto heels. "I was going to ask why you were up so early, but maybe I should change it to why you're out so late!"

"Well, I wanted to see you today, so I figured why not do it now, while I'm fresh. Then when I go home, I can sleep until tomorrow." She headed for the kitchen and the coffee pot, with Sloane close behind.

"I'm almost afraid to ask, but where have you been?"

"The most fabulous party," Carol replied, holding onto her mug as if it were a lifeline. "But only for the sake of my career, of course. Do you know William Edgemont?"

"Who doesn't? Want an omelet?" As they talked, Sloane poured the eggs into a heated pan and popped the bread into the toaster. "Now what about Edgemont?"

"You must have heard about that positively monstrous place he's built. We've been running

155

ourselves ragged all week decorating it. Last night was the housewarming, and in appreciation for our efforts, we peons were invited.'' She sat at the table and watched Sloane deftly fold the omelet over on itself. ''God, you're good. Mine always come out looking like rubber doggie-do.''

''Well, some of us got it, some of us ain't,'' quipped Sloane, sliding the fluffy concoction onto a plate. ''So, what went on with the jet set last night?'' She had heard about Denver's homegrown tycoon, the extravagant lifestyle, and wild parties.

''Oh, the usual tralala. Several of our more prominent citizens made prime asses of themselves; I think it must be the standard ritual for these affairs. But it was fun. And the men! You just wouldn't believe the variety! In fact, I have dates with two of them next Friday night. Would you care to take one of them off my hands?'' With an air of studied innocence, Carol opened her eyes wide, waiting for Sloane's reply.

''If I thought you were serious, I'd stuff toast up your nose. Don't you know by now your match-making won't work? It'll be a long time before I forgive you for that little fiasco with Santee. That was a dirty trick, Carol.''

Carol took the rebuke in good-natured silence, although she looked anything but repentant. ''Speaking of Lucas . . .'' she began.

''We weren't and we won't.''

''All right, don't fly into a tizzy. Actually, I wanted to talk to you on a professional level. Van

Buren and I had quite a discussion about you last night."

"And?"

"And he wants to meet with you at eleven Monday morning instead of two. He's arranged a luncheon meeting with one of our clients. You're on your way to the big time, darling. You'll surely get a commission out of it; and after the exhibition, you'll have more work than you can handle. He's really promoting you."

Sloane didn't know whether to smile or bite her nails. "A commission already? Has this client seen any of my work? Carol, I'm really just an amateur. I know practically nothing about the business, and I've never done anything to someone else's specifications. If this client is really important, maybe van Buren would be wiser to let another sculptor handle it."

"Sweetie, you're worried for nothing. Getting a commission doesn't mean you have to chisel from a blueprint. He'll just tell you what *sort* of thing he wants or whether it's for his home or an office, you know. He'll probably be at the opening, so he'll know for sure if he likes your stuff before he actually commissions you to do anything. Speaking of which, it's only a few weeks away."

"Don't remind me. Every time I think about it, my stomach knots up. Carol, so much depends on this. Snowcrest might think I'm the greatest thing since pantyhose, but Denver's another world." It was a relief to admit her nervousness aloud; for days she'd worked feverishly to prepare for the exhibit, at the same time shying away from thinking about the actual event. "I love what I do, and I'm proud of my work. But every time I think of all those people judging me . . ."

"Stage fright, darling. You've an exceptional talent, and you'll do fine. If van Buren likes you, the rest of the world won't be far behind. And he does like you, believe me. He asked me why, with your talent, you weren't writing your own ticket in the big time."

Sloane, embarrassed by the unsolicited praise, laughed self-consciously. "Give me a break! I've only been at it a few years."

"That's what I told him. And then he got *really* excited." Carol cocked her head to one side with an inquiring look at Sloane. "There's something I've wondered about, honey. Three years ago you were—what?—twenty-eight? Why did you wait so long? You must have been aware of your own talent."

"That's oversimplifying it a bit," she shrugged. "Let's just say I was aware of my own interest in the art. I played around with clay when I was a kid, then when I was in high school my foster parents encouraged me to enter several local contests. I even won a scholarship. So I didn't exactly wake up one day, pick up a carving tool, and make a miracle."

"Then what happened?" Carol persisted. "With

a degree and a major talent, you waited years to put it all into practice.''

''No mystery. I got married.''

Carol gave a most unladylike snort of derision. ''Lots of women get married, dear. It isn't synonymous with death.''

''Michael was a lawyer with his eye on politics. His career was my career, and I just let my own interests get absorbed. I was his hostess, his spokesperson. There were parties, luncheons, speeches, rallies—it was a very full, very busy life. I just didn't have time for sculpting.''

''Feel free to shut me up anytime, but I have to pry a little. What really went wrong in your marriage? It just seems so weird that you two could sail happily along for five years or so, then suddenly come apart at the seams. I can't imagine you, of all people, marrying a man who was so insensitive. He must have had something on the ball, at least in the beginning. I mean, I don't see how he could have been a good guy one day and a bad guy the next. People don't change that quickly.''

Sloane was surprised to realize she no longer felt uncomfortable talking about Michael and her marriage. For so long, the familiar ache of disappointment would oppress her every time she thought about that last horrible day, the day Rena died. But now she was ready to face it head-on. When had she finally let go of the hurt?

''You're right. People don't change that quickly. I guess the simplest way to describe it is that our marriage was a case of mistaken identity. I saw what I wanted to see in Michael; he offered me security, a home of my own, a place where I belonged. And if I ever admitted to myself that I wasn't really in love with him, I justified it by thinking what I'd given him in return.''

"Which was probably a hell of a lot," returned Carol loyally. "I just won't ever believe you cold-bloodedly married someone for a house and a bank account. You're not the type."

"You're right, up to a point. At that time in my life, I needed security, stability. And I genuinely cared for Michael. Maybe there were no skyrockets, but we shared a warm, comfortable affection. If he didn't recognize that I had ambitions of my own, it was probably because I had never let him know. When we found out that neither of us was what the other thought . . ."

How could it be put into words that would *really* explain to Carol, or to anyone else, the crazy series of events that had led inexorably to the demise of her marriage?

First there had been the small things, the little disillusionments:

"Michael, Dean Loeffler called today. Several of his students asked him about private instruction. He thinks I should consider doing it. He thinks it would be a perfect starting point."

"For what? You aren't seriously considering it? Your career is to be beside me, supporting me, being first lady of the state someday."

"I have an art degree, Michael. I'd like to use it, use my mind, my talent."

"I didn't marry you for your degree, darling. You're going to be much too busy just being my wife. Tell Loeffler you aren't interested."

A year or so later, she'd made her first slip:

"Sloane, we're having a small dinner party next week. Grady Halloran is an influential party member; we're trying to get his backing for my campaign." And he thought: *Promise him immunity from prosecution and he'll be in my pocket.*

"Prosecution? For what? I thought he was a respectable businessman? And how can you promise him immunity? Michael, you've sworn to uphold the law! I can't believe it!"

He had stared at her open-mouthed. "Where did you hear that?"

"From you. Just now." It was too late to bluff it out.

He'd said nothing further . . . then. That had come later, when they began arguing about how to handle the letters and phone calls. Sloane wanted to go to the police; Michael adamantly refused.

"Do you have any idea what this kind of publicity could do to me, Sloane? My party is conservative, *ultra*-conservative. The only publicity they want is planned well in advance. The men who make the decisions aren't apt to appreciate the fact that I can't keep my own wife out of the headlines."

"Michael, that's ridiculous! I'm not the criminal! How could it hurt your public image if your wife upholds justice?'' Then, abruptly, she had understood. ''It's Halloran, isn't it? If I'm in the headlines, then so are you, and then, sooner or later, so is he. And he can't stand the scrutiny, he and his crooked friends!''

''You little idiot!'' he had snarled. ''This is my career you're tampering with, and I don't intend to let you take it away from me.''

Sloane had pulled herself up to her full height, closing her throat to the threatening tears. ''You make me sick, Michael. I'm your wife. I believe I'm in danger. Maybe it really is nothing, but you can't be sure of that. I need your help, your protection, and all you can think about is your damned campaign!''

The air in the room had seemed to crackle with tension. Michael's face had distorted with anger, frightening Sloane with its intensity. ''Your revulsion couldn't possibly be any greater than my own. Or have you forgotten how you gained your knowledge of my political allies? Crawling around in my mind, sneaking and probing, violating my very thoughts. To be quite honest, this has merely provided me with the excuse I've needed. When the campaign is over, I'll be more than happy to help you pack. Once I'm elected, I can do without you. You're a monstrous freak, Sloane, and I refuse to live with you creeping around in my head like a grave robber.''

She had fled then, covering her ears, but his voice had echoed on and on.

"Earth calling Sloane . . ."

"What? Oh, Carol, I'm sorry. I was just—remembering." Funny, she thought, it doesn't hurt anymore. That ache is finally gone. "It was a slow process. We just didn't see what was actually there, and when reality set in, the marriage fell apart. It was over long before Rena's death. I was going to leave him after the election."

"Oh, honey, I didn't mean to dredge up unhappy memories for you. I'm sorry." Carol hugged her friend, distressed by Sloane's own anguish. "I swear, I think my mouth gets bigger every day."

"No, it's okay. It's not that painful anymore. And I probably need to be reminded of the reality. Michael's making noises that sound a lot like 'reconciliation.' I have to admit, sometimes it's very tempting."

"The woman's lost her mind! It must be cabin fever." Carol's incredulous expression reflected her thoughts far more clearly than mere words. "Sloane, you aren't really, *seriously* considering going back to him!"

"I guess not." Sloane smiled rather sadly. "Just feeling sorry for myself, I guess, having to face all this mess on my own, and the complications with Santee. Sometimes . . ."

"Sometimes you should get away from this shrine to nature and make half an effort to be sociable. There are plenty of men out there who would jump at the chance to make you forget Michael, and they'd probably do a pretty thorough job of it."

Then Carol's eyes became slyly knowing. "Or is it really Michael you have on your mind? Lucas is pretty unforgettable, isn't he? And I've a hunch you're afraid of him or afraid of what you feel. So going back to Michael would solve the problem very neatly. Trade the unknown for the known, unsatisfying as it might be . . ."

Before the sentence was finished, Sloane had taken the fur coat from its hook beside the front door and extended it meaningfully toward the other woman. "Don't you think it's a little past your bedtime?"

"No, but apparently you do," the blonde countered. "And never let it be said I can't take a hint." She buttoned the coat snugly around her neck. "Thanks for breakfast."

"Sure. And I'll talk to you Monday, after I've met with your boss."

Sloane watched Carol dash for her car, a sporty black number as incongruous in this setting as Carol herself. After her friend drove away, Sloane was aware of a sharp pang of loneliness. Most of the time she wouldn't trade her solitude for anything. But more and more often lately she found herself glancing uneasily out the windows or starting violently at the most ordinary sounds. Her senses seemed to be gearing up for defensive action—but against what? Chapman was still in Dallas; there had been no more phone calls. She was safe now.

Then why was she afraid to be alone?

*   *   *

His plans were nearly complete now. Only twenty-four hours to wait before he could begin.

They all thought they were so smart, following him around, convinced he didn't know they were there. But he had fooled them good. She probably thought she was safe. She'd find out, though. No one was safe from his retribution.

He could feel the power gathering around him, the dark energy buoying him up, helping and strengthening him. Yes, it was almost time. A feeling somewhat like sexual arousal brushed him, and he smiled into the darkness of the dirty room, picturing her face as it would look when she died.

Chapter Eight

IT WAS NEARLY dark when the knock sounded, loud and demanding and most unwelcome.

After Carol had gone, Sloane had finally taken her walk, an exhausting trek covering miles of forest, and she was just out of the shower, clad only in an ankle-length terry robe.

She knew who it was. For a moment, she considered simply ignoring him. If she refused to open the door, maybe he'd go away. But that was a futile hope; Santee wouldn't give up that easily. By the time she reached the door, the knocking had evolved into a forceful reverberation.

When she swung open the door, he was standing there, tall and broad, filling the doorway as well as her senses. Even through her rising anger, she was acutely aware of her weakening defenses. Just the sight of him brought back every move, every whispered word of their mutual seduction only a few days before. But the seduction had ended painfully, as all their encounters seemed to; she stiffened with resolve.

He must have seen her intention even before she could put it into action, for he braced the door with his hand. "If you try to close me out, I'll break it down," he growled. His steely gray eyes glinted dangerously.

"I told you I didn't want to see you again. I meant it." *Liar, even when he hurts you, you want him.* "Will you please leave?"

He stepped inside, closing the door behind him. "You're kidding yourself, Sloane. You don't want me to go away. You've spent the last few days thinking about me, even if you won't admit it. Now why don't we cut the games and do a little honest communicating?"

She gave an angry cough of laughter that wasn't convincing, even to her own ears. "What a switch! I didn't think honest communication was in your repertoire. Intimidation is more your style."

With an expressive gesture, he tossed the ever-present Stetson in the general direction of the sofa. "Damn it, listen to yourself! You're acting like a child, working yourself up over something you think, not what actually is! Now will you sit down and talk to me?"

"Do I have a choice?"

"No."

She chose a spot on the floor, as far away from the sofa as she could get. "All right, talk."

His long frame was out of place on the soft floral print of the deep cushions, but it didn't matter. He looked at her for a long moment before he spoke again.

"There's a lot I want to say. But I'll start with the worst and you'd better-by-God listen. I won't say you were wrong about what I was feeling that day, after Michael's call—I'm not sure you were wrong. But you were mistaken about my motives. Sloane, I'm just a man. I can't help my feelings about Chapman. Maybe I did have some macho visions of beating him to death and taking great pleasure in it, but I won't apologize for that. He's caused too much grief for me to give up my dreams of revenge that easily." His gaze bored into hers, compelling her to meet his eyes and respond to his logic. "But I did *not,* not once, ever consider using you to get to him. And that's what you thought, wasn't it?"

Under the directness of his scrutiny, she had to answer, "Yes."

"And you also thought my anger and bitterness was because of Rena. Well, you're right, up to a point. A month ago it would have been absolutely true. But now it's for you, too, now that I know what he put you through . . . is still putting you through. I've never wanted to kill anyone before, Sloane, but I want to kill Chapman. He's already taken one person I love and damned near took another. Do you understand what I'm saying?''

She wanted to understand, wanted to desperately, but the fear of disappointment was smothering. ''All I know is that when Michael called to tell me I was safe, out of danger, you weren't happy for me. That only leaves one possibility. You *wanted* Chapman to come here, to come for me . . .''

His irritation showed in the quick, angry shake of his head. ''No. It wasn't like that. If you want me to put into words what I was feeling—yes, I guess I did want Chapman here. But only to protect you. If he's here, we can stop him, get to him first. As long as he's in Texas, there'll always be the possibility he'll just pop up someday. Don't you see? I want to keep you, Sloane, alive and well and loving. . . . Sloane, look at me. I love you.''

She couldn't see him clearly because of the tears, but she tried.

He was kneeling in front of her, his hands on her arms, drawing her close. ''Don't cry. Don't ever cry again.''

She drew back, twisting away from him. His touch might trigger the psi, and she didn't want to know what he was thinking. She wanted to learn to trust in what he said; she needed that kind of normalcy. For now, his words were enough.

But it wasn't enough for Santee. He captured her hands in his own. ''You're trembling.''

"I know," she whispered. "I'm scared."

"Of me? Or Chapman?"

"Both of you. You both torment me. And I don't think I can take much more."

He hugged her tightly against his chest; his heartbeat was steady, soothing. "Sweet Sloane," he murmured huskily. "Stop fighting me. Love me instead."

When their lips met, passion flared through them both like a tangible flame. She was dizzy with the intensity of the feelings he aroused, bereft when he lifted his mouth from hers.

"How do you do this to me?" she whispered shakily.

His laugh was low but unsteady. "We do it to each other. Hadn't you noticed?"

She swayed against him again, wanting him with a painful ache. "Stay with me tonight?"

In answer, he crushed her slender body to his. His kiss told her everything she needed to know. Then, their minds touched. She fought to clamp down on it, tried to use the shielding discipline she'd learned so many years ago, but it was futile. The love, strong and enduring, radiated between them, blinding in its sweet intensity, seducing her with its purity.

Like a breaking glass, the intimacy between them shattered with the discordant jangle of the telephone. Sloane flinched, uttering a small cry, at the same time clutching at his sleeves with clammy hands.

"I'm sorry," she said, swallowing hard. "I don't know why I'm so keyed up lately."

She answered on the third ring.

"Hello?"

A chilly, hissing silence was the only response. Her skin crawled and she shivered. A tentacle of fear encircled her heart and squeezed.

"Hello? Who is it?"

From very far away there came a faint sound, as of someone laughing quietly.

"Who is this? Answer me!" She heard the rising panic in her voice and bit down on her tongue.

The long-distance laugh became clearer, a note of pure pleasure that terrified her. The voice was slow and deliberate. *"Your time is up."*

She slammed the receiver back into its cradle, feeling as if she'd been bitten by a particularly vicious and deadly snake. Santee was instantly beside her, holding her shoulders, supporting her as she sagged.

"What's wrong?" When she didn't answer, he shook her once, alarmed at her pallor. "Damnit, Sloane, what happened?"

"It was Chapman," she finally answered dully. "He said my time was up. He'll be here soon . . ."

"No. No, he won't, love." Very tenderly, with infinite care, he held her close and kissed her face and eyes, smoothing her hair back. "I'll keep you safe. It's all right."

She burrowed into the warmth of his chest and sighed tremulously, her hands groping for the security to be found in the feel of his strong body. "Don't leave me tonight, Santee. Don't talk about it, any of it, but stay with me."

He lifted her effortlessly and carried her upstairs. Deep into the night, they loved again and again, until her demons were exorcised and, at last, she slept.

Santee wakened at dawn. Nestled against him, her head resting in the curve of his shoulder, Sloane began to toss fitfully, sometimes murmuring words he couldn't understand, occasionally whimpering as she fled from the nightmare specter. Once he started to slip out of bed, intending to call Will Lambert at home, but even in sleep she reached out to him for reassurance, and he couldn't bring himself to leave her.

In the early light, her face was pale and perfect, her lovely mouth so vulnerable; he felt a sudden wave of anger that she should feel even one moment of fear or despair. He had never before been so inescapably bound to another person, so irrevocably committed. Somehow, Sloane Taylor had become the focus of his life; her pain was now his personal concern.

The hatred he had previously felt for Chapman had grown until it was no longer recognizable as a single emotion. It was black and twisted, filling Santee with such a powerful need for action that his fists clenched unconsciously and spasmodically.

Next to him, Sloane stirred again, sighing. He

waited until she was still, then slipped carefully out of bed and pulled on his jeans and shirt. Before he left the bedroom, he pulled the blanket snugly around her shoulders, then kissed her gently.

Downstairs, he puttered around in the kitchen, waiting until he was certain Will Lambert was in his office. He found coffee makings, plugged in the pot, wandered into the living room and poked absently at the dead coals in the fireplace, found a weather report on the radio, and listened to it while he drank his first cup of coffee.

At last it was seven o'clock. He dialed the number of the Snowcrest Sheriff's Office and wasted no time when Lambert came on the line.

"I want you to call Texas, Will. Find out exactly where Gerald Chapman is and what he's doing. And get hold of Michael Fielding. Tell him to have Chapman trailed round the clock."

"If you say so, Luke. Something happened, did it?"

"He called Sloane last night—scared her senseless, said her 'time was up.' "

"Could be he's just getting his kicks, but there's no point in taking chances. I'll make the calls and get back to you."

"I think there's more to it, Will. Sloane's not the kind to overreact, go all hysterical unless she's got a damn good reason. I trust her instincts about this."

"Why don't you talk to her about having her number changed? Better yet, see if you can get her to move. It's pretty hard to protect her when she lives that far out.''

"Yeah, I know,'' Santee said. "I'm working on it. I'd like her to come out to the ranch, but I've got a feeling she'll be stubborn about it.''

Lambert chuckled. "Sounds like you've got a bad case, friend. Reminds me of high school. Remember Laura Jean?''

"Yeah.'' For two years, he and Laura Jean Phillips had been the hottest thing at Snowcrest High School. When she dropped him for a senior linebacker, Santee had laid it all on his friend, Will Lambert. "Let's hope Sloane doesn't have a football fetish.''

"You got a permanent arrangement on your mind?''

"It's beginning to look that way,'' Santee replied wryly. "Now all I have to do is talk her into it. And the sooner the better, with Chapman creeping around.''

"Right. I'll let you know what turns up. And don't worry. We'll start patrolling out there again if Chapman's not where he's supposed to be.''

After he hung up, Santee poured another cup of coffee, then went into the living room just in time to see Sloane come down the stairs. She was looking down, her face partly obscured by the veil of long chestnut hair hanging in soft waves past her shoulders. Her delicate features were still pale, emphasized by the shadows beneath her eyes. All

Santee's protective instincts surfaced, and he stepped toward her, speaking softly.

"Should you be up so early? You know you didn't get much sleep last night."

When she blushed, he realized what she must be thinking. "No, love, that's not what I meant. Although I can't think of a better way to pass the time." He kissed her lightly. "I just meant you didn't rest well. Why don't you go back to bed?"

She shook her head. "I have to go into Denver this morning to meet with Mr. van Buren about the exhibit. And I need to make some phone calls."

"I've already talked to Will Lambert. Let's fix breakfast and I'll tell you about it."

She laid her hand on his arm. "Thank you for being here. I needed you last night."

"Only last night?" he teased. Then, sensing her withdrawal, he added, "We'll talk about last night later. How about some coffee?"

Exhausted and unsure how to handle the situation, which seemed to have created more problems than it solved, she allowed him to pamper her, accepting his obvious love and concern without a word to betray her inner turmoil.

While Santee made himself at home in her kitchen, cooking breakfast and reassuring her that Lambert was checking out the situation in Texas, part of her mind was replaying the tormenting dreams of the past night. She knew he attributed her fatigue and depression to Chapman's call and the emotional aftermath of her fear. And that was true, at least partly true.

She had been calmed, comforted, and transported by his lovemaking. Sweet and savage by turns, it had been the single most incredible experience of her life. And that was the problem. It was her love for Santee—and his for her—that had caused the nightmares. She wanted to explain it to him, make him understand how wrong it would be to prolong a relationship which was doomed to failure, but she couldn't find the words.

If ever there had been a one-woman man, it was Santee. She knew he had given her a rare and wonderful gift—his love—and without it, her life would be cold and lonely. But she'd better get used to it.

Already, Santee was thinking in terms of marriage and children, and that was what had haunted her sleep: dreams of love shriveling into hatred once he discovered what she was. No one could, or should, live with the knowledge that their thoughts and emotions could never again be private, that at any time their mind could be invaded by another, even if it were someone they loved. And children, of course, were out of the question. Her affliction was apparently genetic; any child of hers would surely be destined to suffer the same fears, frustration, and aloneness that had always tortured her.

". . . think you should move, honey. It's too dangerous for you to be out here alone. You'll be moving to the ranch anyway, after we're married. Why not do it now?''

''No!'' She hadn't meant to sound so abrupt; she went on hurriedly, ''Santee, there's something I have to explain to you . . .''

''I agree,'' he interrupted. ''We do have things to discuss, but somehow I get the impression it won't be to my liking.'' He set two plates of food on the table along with the coffeepot, then seated himself opposite her. ''But right now, we're going to eat breakfast, then you're going to get ready for your meeting with van Buren. Tonight we'll talk.''

She didn't force a discussion, recognizing the implacability in his tone. It would be better, anyway, to wait. Right now she wasn't capable of handling what must be said with the self-control and care that would be needed. Tonight would be much better. Maybe tonight she could make him understand.

It was sleeting lightly, coating the roads with an invisible, treacherous layer of ice. She passed several accidents on the way into Denver, and traffic was somewhat slow; but she had allowed herself ample time for the drive and walked into the gallery precisely at eleven.

The lunch meeting with van Buren and his client, Richard Ellis, went quite well, Sloane thought. Both men seemingly approved of her suggestions for accent pieces to highlight Mr. Ellis' new offices. She had sketched a few of her ideas for them and made notes on Ellis' description of the decor, and they'd made an appointment for her to have a firsthand look at the building next week. To her surprise, he even asked if she would work up some drawings from which he could choose a Christmas gift for his wife.

The only awkward moment occurred when she told Ellis she wouldn't start work on his project until after the exhibit. Van Buren's stormy expression told her she had made a tactical error, and after Ellis left the table, he expressed his displeasure in no uncertain terms.

"He said he wouldn't be surprised if Ellis took his business to someone who would be more 'accommodating,' " she told Carol later, after van Buren had spent an hour with her in his office, going over the contracts he'd drawn up.

"Uh-oh, bad way to start the day. What'd you do?"

"Something terrible. I was rude to him, Carol. I told him if he didn't like the way I conducted business, he could look for another protégé."

"You didn't!"

"I did. I guess my nerves just finally snapped. Anyway, he glared at me, then he laughed, and then he said he thought we'd get along just fine together."

"Why that old bully!" Carol exclaimed. "For years I've been tiptoeing around his bad temper, and all I needed to do was shout back at him!"

"Well, let's just say it worked this time."

"Of course it did. You're worth a lot of money to him. If Ellis commissions you to do his new office building, the gallery gets a hefty fee, and there's been a lot of interest in those pieces of yours he got from Margaret Johanssen. He wouldn't be much of a businessman if he let you get away. Oops, got a customer. 'Bye, sweetie. Be careful. It's *nasty* outside."

On the way out of the gallery, Sloane paused beside one of her sculptures. It was almost like seeing it through a stranger's eyes for the very first time. *It really is good,* she thought. But would it be enough to fill up an empty life?

Driving out of the city was slow and tedious work. The sleet had turned to snow, and the white stuff was piling up at an alarming rate. She had the windshield wipers going at top speed while she inched along the city streets.

The highway wasn't quite so bad, although she passed two more accidents, and in several places snowplows had traffic backed up in their attempts to keep pace with the worsening snowfall. The intermittent radio reports she heard held out a fifty-fifty chance the skies would start clearing by the next day, but the forecasters didn't sound too optimistic. Looking at the lowering sky, she didn't blame them.

At least the temperature was up a few degrees, she reflected, so there was little danger of a hard freeze. She hated the thought of trying to navigate the light sports car over icy roads. Even at her best, winter driving made her nervous. And she was far from her best today. As tired as she was, she shouldn't even be driving; in weather like this she could be a criminal menace.

A few miles out of town, the road conditions improved and she was able to pick up a little speed. Apparently the road crews had already been through, scraping and salting. At any rate, she felt she could relax a notch or two. In her condition, it was sheer hard effort to concentrate on driving or on anything else. For a while, fired with enthusiasm for the upswing in her professional life, she had managed to throw off most of her fatigue and low spirits, but alone in the small car with only a radio for company, it was all too easy for the problems to come flooding back.

As she left the city behind, she wearily replayed it all, starting with Gerald Chapman. No matter what anyone said to the contrary, Sloane knew it was only a matter of time before Chapman would come for her. She had seen his eyes, felt his hands on her—she had known his insane thoughts. He wouldn't give up, and he would never be satisfied with simple long-distance harassment. He wanted her dead. There were times when she could feel him, like a physical presence, an intruder in her space.

And he threatened not only her but Santee as well. Once Chapman got within striking range, Santee was sure to be in the thick of it. If Chapman were an ordinary foe, that would have been a comforting thought. As it was, she very much feared for Santee's safety.

"Even without Chapman, it would be a mess," she said aloud, starting at the unexpected sound of her voice in the confines of the small car. "Great! Now I'm talking to myself."

But why shouldn't I? she thought then. *Who else can I talk to? Okay,* she decided, *let's have a go at auto-therapy.* At least it would keep her awake.

What's the basic problem, Miss Taylor?

"Santee. He wants marriage, a family, a future."

And how do you feel about that?

"It would be wrong. It would be tragic."

Why? Don't you love him?

"Oh, yes. More than anything."

Then why not marry him?

"Because it wouldn't be fair."

To whom?

"To him. He doesn't know everything. And when he finds out, he'll despise me; so it wouldn't be fair to me either, to have to give him up after just a little while."

But wouldn't a few years, even a few months with him be worth the pain?

"That's not a fair question. There's more at stake . . ." She pressed her fingertips against her burning eyes, closing them for just a moment. When she opened them again, the road was blurry, slightly out of focus. At the edge of her vision, a tentative movement became a deer, bounding directly in front of the car.

She hit the brakes.

The skid spun the car around once, then twice, and she sickened. The third time sent her onto the shoulder to careen off the guardrail. The car rolled onto its side with a crunch, teetering at the top of a steep embankment on the opposite side of the highway.

Sloane felt the impact as her head struck the side window. She didn't feel a thing when the eastbound truck clipped the rear of her car, sending it tumbling down on a large outcropping of rock.

The Greyhound station in Dallas was crowded, as always, and no one paid much attention to the shabbily dressed man who paid for his ticket with small bills and change.

He sat in the very back of the bus, in comforting solitude and darkness, his lips working as he talked to himself. It was so easy to confuse them, the fools. They wouldn't even know he was gone until the next day, and that was all the head start he needed.

He stroked the knife. *Sleep tight, Mrs. Fielding.*

Chapter Nine

THE LIGHT WAS much too bright, even through closed eyelids, and the antiseptic smell too strong. The odor was familiar, but for the moment she couldn't recall what it reminded her of, except that it wasn't pleasant. Her stomach rolled; she was on the verge of disgracing herself, and that thought made her more miserable than ever. The effort of trying to lift her head set off a pneumatic drill in her skull and she groaned.

"Sloane? Are you awake, honey?"

Oh, it was good to hear his voice. For some reason she couldn't remember right now, she was scared. Knowing Santee was here made it easier.

She tried to open her eyes, but it hurt, and the nausea was getting worse. "I'm sick," she whispered. "I need to get up . . ."

Strong hands pressed her shoulders against the pillow. "Lie still, honey. The doctor's on his way."

"Doctor? Why? What's wrong?" *Why was she hurting so? Something had happened—why couldn't she remember?*

"You're all right now. You were in an accident and you've been out for a while. But it's not serious. You're going to be fine."

This time she managed to open her eyes a fraction. She couldn't see his face clearly, but his voice was steady, comforting. "Was anyone else hurt?"

"No. The only fatality was your car. Now lie still. Try not to worry."

It was easy to obey. The pain was less acute if she didn't move, didn't think. From a distance, she heard another voice telling Santee she would probably sleep some more, that he should go home and come back tomorrow. Santee refused. She was glad, even if it was selfish. As long as he was with her, she would be all right.

Santee stopped the doctor by the nurse's station. "Are you sure she's okay? She seemed to be in a lot of pain."

The doctor smiled indulgently. "The pain is to be expected, Mr. Santee. If the first bump on the head were the only injury, she'd have been out of here by now. But she received quite a shake-up in the second accident—more blows to the head, a

184

twisted neck, and her right shoulder is severely wrenched. She has a concussion and several bruised ribs.''

''When can she go home?'' Santee had no quarrel with the care she had received so far, but he'd feel better when he could take her home to Crooked Creek and look after her himself.

''Because of the concussion, we'd like to keep her at least forty-eight hours. If she feels up to it, we'll discharge her Wednesday afternoon or Thursday morning.''

Santee hurried back to room 255. Sloane was sleeping. Wearily, he dropped into the chair beside her and slumped down, letting his head fall back.

He still wasn't quite over the shock. Will's call had stunned him. Sloane, involved in an accident, something about a diesel rig. And she'd been taken to a hospital in Denver. Will didn't know how serious her injuries were, only that she'd been unconscious when she was pulled from her car. In his rush to Denver, he'd passed the wrecker on the highway. *Christ!* he'd thought, seeing the mangled wreckage of the little sports car. *How had she lived through it?* She was so slender, so delicate, and the car was crumpled like a discarded beer can.

His heart hadn't slowed until he saw her for himself, pale and bandaged, but breathing evenly. She'd looked small and forlorn in the hospital bed, her skin nearly as white as the sheets. But she was alive; he hadn't lost her. In his relief, he'd cried for the first time since his father died.

During the hours he'd sat in the waiting room while she was being examined, x-rayed, and tested, he had done some hard thinking—about Sloane and how much she had come to mean to him, about himself and his future. One thing was certain, he'd decided. Whatever it took, he would have her beside him. It wouldn't be easy. She was wary of entanglements, commitments. Part of the problem was her rotten marriage to Michael Fielding. But there was more to it. Maybe it had something to do with her uniqueness, her strange talent, whatever it was called. It was the damnedest thing, the way she'd known what he was thinking that day. He didn't have it figured out yet, but he would. And whatever it was, it didn't matter. He could accept it, had already accepted it.

But he would have to break through the shell she had grown, and when he did he would win her. She already loved him, he was convinced of that. There was too much magic between them, the kind of oneness that couldn't be faked, a deepness more enduring than passion. Oh, he knew it would be tough. There were problems, plenty of them, but he'd work them out—starting with Chapman.

His rage over Rena's murder hadn't lessened, but it had changed direction. Getting to Chapman wouldn't bring Rena back. But it would protect

Sloane. If it took all his time, all his strength, his very life, that animal would never harm her again.

With a gentle finger, he traced the thin scar on her neck and trembled with fury. She had risked her life to help catch his sister's killer, all alone with no one to love or protect her. Had it not been for Will Lambert, he never would have known. Whatever the price, he vowed, she'd never suffer like that again.

It was late, nearly midnight, when she awoke once more. Her head still throbbed, but the nausea had eased considerably and her vision was better. Beside her, slumped in a chair that looked decidedly uncomfortable, Santee dozed, his long frame sprawled untidily in several directions. Her heart turned over with love as she recognized the bedside vigil, the weariness evident in his drawn features.

"Hey, cowboy, it's time to go home," she said softly, noting the unsteadiness of her own voice.

He blinked, then smiled. "Welcome back. I was beginning to worry."

"Worry, my foot," she teased. "You were asleep. But I forgive you. What time is it?"

"Five to twelve. Do you need anything? I'll call the nurse."

"In a minute. Is it still Monday?" For all she knew, she could have been here for days.

"Barely. You've been out quite a while. Do

you remember what happened?'' He took her hand, relieved to find it warm, normal.

''Some of it. There was a deer, I think—the car skidded. It's fuzzy, though. Did I hurt anybody?''

''You asked that before. No, even the deer got away. Your car flipped a couple of times, then a truck hit it, but the driver's not hurt. The car's a mess, though. We'll get you a new one when you're able to drive.'' He stood up and pressed the call light for the nurse. ''You probably need to take some medication, so I'll grab a cup of coffee and come back when they're through poking around on you.''

''No. I want you to go home.'' He looked so tired and worn. Knowing he'd spent the past seven or eight hours worried about her was both warming and distressing. She felt like such a weasel, accepting his love and concern while all the time she was planning to leave him.

''I'd rather stay.'' His tone clearly told of the anxieties of the past day.

''Please. I'd just worry about you, scrunched up in a chair all night.''

''Okay.'' He kissed her. ''But I'll be back early tomorrow morning.'' At the door, he looked back. ''Sloane? I love you.''

She nodded. *I love you, too.* ''I know.''

''Good night, honey.''

Tuesday morning was hazy. The pain medication had built up in her system, keeping her in an uneasy doze. She woke briefly when Santee entered the room, but drifted off again, aware of his comforting presence, his hand holding hers. It wasn't until early afternoon that she felt like taking an interest in what was going on around her, and even then she was content to be a passive observer rather than a participant.

When Will Lambert walked in, she was propped up for the first time, cautiously sipping a glass of tomato juice. He was ill at ease, as most men are in the company of an ill or injured woman, and he stayed only a few minutes before asking Santee to join him outside.

"We got some information on those trespassers you mentioned the other day, Lucas, if you've got a minute to talk."

A brief look passed between the two men, and fleetingly she wondered what male secrets they were conspiring to keep from her. But as they left the room, Carol breezed in, loaded with flowers, magazines, and a small, oddly colored bottle, claiming Sloane's full attention with her usual exuberance.

"How are you, sweetie? Sorry I didn't get here sooner. I did peek in last night, while you were asleep. The old man sends his regards and felicitations, etcetera, and wants to know if you'll be ready for the opening on time."

They laughed at van Buren's typical preoccupation with the gallery, and Sloane replied, "Tell him it'll take more than a few bumps and bruises to keep me from my destiny. What are you loaded down with?''

''I can tell you from experience there is nothing more boring than being stuck in a bed, alone, so I brought you some diversionary materials.''

Glancing over the items Carol laid on the bed, Sloane grinned. ''It's a touching gesture, Carol, and I really do appreciate the thought. But what exactly am I supposed to do with all these back issues of *Nudists on Parade* and a bottle of lime-green nail polish?''

''Improvise, darling. It's an exercise in imagination.''

As Carol settled down for what promised to be a long chat, Sloane tried to relax and enjoy her friend's lively banter. But her gaze kept straying to the closed door of her room. Santee and Lambert had been gone a long time.

''They're absolutely sure of their information?'' Santee was asking. ''No chance they've made a mistake?''

''Not according to Fielding,'' Will replied. ''He had his detectives make the rounds of bus stations and airports with Chapman's picture. He was positively identified by two Greyhound employees. Caught the two a.m. bus in Dallas.''

''What time will that put him in Denver?''

The sheriff shook his head. ''Can't even be sure this is where he's headed. Fielding checked the schedule. If he is coming this way, he'd have to change buses in Abilene, Lubbock, and Amarillo, or he could have got off anywhere in between.''

"Can't be sure?" Santee exploded. "You know damn well he's on his way! Can't you watch the bus terminal and have him picked up?"

"On what charge?" Will felt as Santee did; he'd lay odds Gerald Chapman would show up here in the next twenty-four hours, but his hands were tied. "The man hasn't done anything, Lucas. Besides, he'd be a fool to stick to that bus schedule. He may be crazy, but he's not stupid. He'll only ride so far, then he'll rent a car or maybe hitchhike the rest of the way. We can't stop every car coming into Denver.''

Santee had never felt so helpless, so impotent. "Then you're telling me you can't do anything until he tries to kill her again. The law is on *his* side!''

"If it were any different, we'd have a police state, Lucas. Besides, a half-smart lawyer could get him out of jail in no time on a false arrest charge. He has to *do* something before we can pick him up. Now you know we'll do everything we can to protect her. My boys drive out by her place every day, and from now on they'll check it more often. It won't be that easy for him. He can't find her without asking questions, and in Snowcrest, that'll get around quick. The important thing is not to leave her alone.''

"I'm going to take her back to the ranch when

191

she's discharged, but she'll want to go home as soon as she can. She's a stubborn woman."

"Do you want me to tell her? She'll be wondering what's going on."

Santee sighed, rubbing the back of his neck to ease the tension. "No, not yet. She doesn't need to worry about anything right now, not while she's in this shape. Let her think everything's okay. She'll find out soon enough."

"Maybe sooner than you think." Lambert looked at his friend sympathetically. "I hate to give you any more bad news, but Fielding's on his way up here. He called me when he couldn't get hold of Sloane, and when he found out about her accident, he said he was flying in tomorrow."

"Damn!" This was one complication he hadn't counted on. After three years, Fielding was suddenly trying to worm his way back into her life, and that could only mean one thing—he wanted her back. Now Santee had two good reasons to hate Fielding. Rena was gone, but he'd be damned if he'd lose Sloane, too.

By Wednesday Sloane was more than ready to go home. It seemed as if she'd been in the hospital for weeks instead of a mere two days.

Through the window Denver sparkled in the sunlight like a new penny, and Sloane could hardly wait to trade this impersonal sterility for crisp, fresh air and the smell of spruce.

The doctor had already been in to see her; now

it was just a matter of going by the business office and signing herself out.

As she brushed her hair, feeling awkward with her right arm in a sling and her neck encased in a bulky brace, she watched Santee gathering up the few personal items Carol had brought her. He'd been beside her almost constantly through this whole thing, and she was dismayed at how dependent she'd become on him in such a short time. She had to end it, and soon. He needed a normal woman, one who could give him normal children. She had to tell him goodbye. The longer she put it off, the harder it would be, but, God, she needed him so!

Thinking about it sent her spiraling into a painful depression. Always, it seemed, she had to fight for her equilibrium where Santee was concerned.

Her spirits improved immensely once they were on the road for home. It was a beautiful day; she was out of the hospital; her injuries would heal. Time enough to think of the other problems later, when she had no choice. She could hardly wait to see her cabin again, touch all the familiar things that were so precious to her.

"I can't believe how excited I am," she almost bubbled. "You'd think I've been away for years. Do you get homesick like that when you have to be away from the ranch?"

He glanced at her uneasily, willing her to give in and accept his reasoning. "Honey, I'm not taking you back to your place. The doctor said you'd be having dizzy spells for a while, and it'll be too hard for you to take care of yourself in a sling and a brace. You should stay at the ranch with me until you're back on your feet."

"Santee, don't try to make my decisions for me." Physical and emotional pain had combined to make her edgy and irritable. "I *am* on my feet. My head still hurts some, but that's all. I haven't had one dizzy spell; I can dress myself and make sandwiches. I want to go home."

"You just don't want to be at the ranch. Sloane, I already know you've got some crazy notion about trying to end it between us. I can do a little mind reading of my own, you know." He ignored her gasp. "That's one of the things we'll hash out when you're stronger. But right now the important thing is for you to get well, and to do that you need someone to look after you."

"You are not going to bully me into this, Santee," she declared, digging in her heels. "I want to go home. If I have any problems, I can stay with Carol. But I'm not going to the ranch."

"Carol works. She wouldn't be there to take care of you. Now why can't you be reasonable?"

"I don't have to be reasonable!" She was close to tears. "I just don't want to see you anymore, and you're trying to move me in with you." She hadn't wanted to say it like that, hadn't wanted to hurt him, but he was pushing her into a corner.

But if he was hurt by her words, he did an admirable job of hiding the trauma. "That's a lie. Not only do you want to see me, you want to marry me and live happily ever after. Whatever fool notions you've got for saying different can wait until some other time."

She stamped her foot angrily, no easy task for an injured woman in a sitting position. "I will not be bullied, Santee! Take me home!"

Coping with her childishness was telling on his nerves, and before he fully realized what he was saying, he had blurted it out: "Damn it! You can't go home! It's not safe!"

"What are you talking about? I just told you, I feel fine."

He sighed, exasperated with them both. "It's not you—it's Chapman. Will Lambert told me yesterday when he came by the hospital." God, he hadn't wanted to tell her yet, especially not like that.

"I don't understand," she whispered. "You said he talked to you about some kids who had been trespassing on your land. You lied to me?"

"That part wasn't a lie, honey," he said, reaching for her hand. "I just didn't tell you the rest. Your ex-husband called Will yesterday morning. When Chapman didn't show up for work, the detectives he hired started looking for him. They found out he'd gotten on a bus late Monday night. We have to assume he's on his way here."

She whimpered softly, a hopeless little sound that wrenched at his insides.

"Why didn't you tell me?"

"I was going to, believe me. But the doctor said

you should stay as quiet and calm as possible. I just wanted to give you time to get stronger.''

She stared through the car window at the scenery whizzing past in a blur. When they passed the cut-off that led up the mountain to her cabin, a shiver of apprehension ran through her already chilled body. *He's waiting for me. And I'm so afraid.*

He stood in the deep shadows of the trees surrounding the A-frame cabin, his coat collar pulled up tightly against the cold. This was it, just where the service station attendant said it would be.

From his pocket he drew a folded newspaper and looked once more at the picture of a wrecked automobile on the bottom of the front page. *So you got banged up a little, huh, Mrs. Fielding? What a shame.*

He was glad she hadn't been killed. That was something he was looking forward to. He wondered when she'd come home. Soon, he hoped. But no matter how long it took, he'd be here, waiting.

Chapter Ten

"I THOUGHT I heard you stirring around. How do you feel this morning?"

"Like Joe Frazier's punching bag." Actually, she thought, the punching bag was probably in better shape. Her neck and shoulder ached abominably with even the slightest movement, and every breath was a painful reminder of the beating her ribs had taken. She hadn't even attempted to get dressed, settling for the heavy robe Santee had left in her room the night before. At least she had managed to get the major tangles out of her hair before he peeked around the door.

"Lucky for you I just happen to be carrying the best all-round prescription for what ails you. Salty's coffee is strong enough to dull a toothache." He placed a carafe and two cups on a table near the window and poured for both of them before sitting on the edge of the bed next to her.

As they sipped at the steaming brew, Sloane was uncomfortably aware of the unspoken tension between them. His face was drawn, and his eyes bespoke a tiredness much deeper than physical fatigue. It was clear neither of them had come any closer to solving their problems during the long and restless night just past.

"Would you like some breakfast?" he asked when several minutes had passed in silence.

"No. I'm not very hungry right now. Maybe later." How should she start? What should she say?

"I've asked Hank's wife to come over later. You'll need some help adjusting the brace and taking a shower. I thought you'd be more comfortable with a woman."

"Thank you." Thank God he wasn't going to force any intimacy on her. Right now it was all she could do not to ask him to hold her, to stay with her forever.

"Sloane, loosen up. We shouldn't be like this with each other. I realize we have some serious talking to do, but it doesn't have to be unpleasant."

"It's already unpleasant. You're going to be angry with me, but I can't put it off any longer." She'd give anything if this day were already over, behind her. It was going to be the saddest day of her life.

"Then don't put it off. Tell me."

"Santee, I want to go home. I mean, I know I can't stay alone until Chapman's found, but I don't want to stay here. I can stay with Carol. . . ."

His mouth tightened. "Honey, we've been through that. For at least the next few days, you shouldn't be alone, and Carol can't quit her job to stay with you. Whatever you've got on your mind about us, can't it wait a week or so? The important thing is to protect you."

"All right, let's talk about Chapman, then," she said, facing him. "I know your feelings—you'd like to be the one to get him. But it's a police matter, Santee. You don't have the right to go after him. And how can you be so sure I'm any safer here with you? If he's managed to track me down from Texas to Colorado, it won't be that hard to find me here on the ranch. Everyone in Snowcrest probably knows by now that I'm staying here with you."

"But we have the advantage," he argued. "There are half a dozen men on this place twenty-four hours a day. He couldn't get within a half-mile of the house without somebody spotting him. Come on, Sloane, you're just making excuses. Let me have the real reasons."

"I don't think I can, not right now," she whispered. Why had this happened to her?

Taking her cup, he disposed of both of them, then put his arms around her gently and pressed her face to his shoulder. "It's not fair to try to shove me out of your life without giving me a reason, sweetheart. I love you, and I know you love me. So if you want me to understand, you'd better start talking.''

She couldn't meet his eyes. ''It's so hard. I can't marry you, Santee. I can't give you the kind of life you want. You're right, I do love you, too much to let this go on any longer. Our—affair—should never have happened.''

''Look at me,'' he murmured, tilting her chin up and kissing her lips softly. ''Whatever deep, dark secrets you have, they don't matter. I love the Sloane Taylor of right now, today. Her problems, as well as her dreams, are my problems and my dreams. I want you just the way you are, honey, warts and all.''

''You don't understand!'' Close to tears, she pushed him away. She had to make him understand, and there was no simple way to tell him. ''I'm not normal, Santee! I *hear* things in people's minds; I know things I shouldn't know, and I can't turn it off!''

''I've already figured that out, honey, at least part of it. And you're right, I don't really understand. But I'm ready to try. And I can accept it because it's part of what you are.'' Lovingly he traced the curve of her cheek.

''No! It's a curse, and I've fought it all my life. Listen to me, Santee. It's genetic.'' Even now she had only to close her eyes to conjure up the nightmares of her childhood. How could she ever convey to him, to anyone, how alone and alienated she had felt? "My mother lost her mind and committed suicide because of it. Her father was the same way; nobody knows what happened to him. He was a lonely, tormented man, and one day he just went away. I can't ever have children. I won't pass this along to another living soul; it would be wrong!"

Her control, so long maintained, was close to the breaking point, and he searched for the words to comfort her. "Then we won't have children. It's *you* I want to spend the rest of my life with. Where did you get the idea I couldn't live without a passel of kids?"

"From you. You see? I've already been in your head, and you didn't even know it. The first day we met, at the diner, I knew. You want two boys and a girl; you want them to grow up here on Crooked Creek like you did; you want to take them fishing in the stream. You've even got their colleges picked out . . ." Her voice trailed off in tears.

"Christ!" He had thought he was prepared, but it was now obvious he hadn't any real perception of the extent of her abilities or of the uncertainty and turmoil she'd had to deal with. "You mean you've been worrying about that all this time? Kids are kids, Sloane. Sure, I had a picture in my head of what I thought the ideal family should be. But that was before. People change, honey; their ideas change. We don't have to have kids of our own. We could adopt. Or if it were just the two of us, together, for the next eighty or ninety years, that would be enough for me. Sloane, I want *you*!''

''You want me *now*,'' she answered stubbornly, ''but that would change. It's easy for you to say you accept it; you've never been through it. I have. Michael couldn't stand it. He called me a freak. And he was right. People have a right to their secrets, Santee, to their privacy. You could never be sure I wasn't eavesdropping on your thoughts; you'd begin to avoid me.'' She choked and couldn't continue.

''Are you telling me you know everything that goes on in my head, Sloane? Because I don't believe that.''

She shook her head. ''It's very erratic, but it's strong. As long as I clamp down on it, I can control most of the reception. But my control isn't perfect. Sometimes things slip by, especially in emotional or intimate situations. Then, before I can block, I'm there, inside your head, listening to things you might not want me to know. And that's horrible, for me and for you.'' She avoided looking at him, unwilling to face what she might see in his face because, put into words, it all sounded quite insane.

''You're selling me short, sweetheart. We could make it if you'd trust me enough to try. Look into my mind now, if you can. I *want* you to know what I'm feeling.''

"I knew you wouldn't understand," she said sadly. "But I've made my decision. I won't take a chance on seeing the disgust in your eyes one day. I just couldn't stand it—it would kill me, and I'm tired of hurting."

He tried to hold her again, but she twisted away. His heart ached for her; he never imagined she had been through so much. Reluctantly he rose from the bed. "Okay, you've had your say. I understand now, but I still think you're wrong. Later, when you're stronger, we'll talk again. I won't give up."

For a long time after he left the room, she lay quietly, letting the past wash over her. If she didn't reinforce her decision with reality, she felt, it would be too easy to give in to false hope. . . .

Sloane remembered her mother as a slight, shadowy figure, always nervous, usually crying, sometimes incoherent. There were "voices" in her head, she claimed, demons who tormented her ceaselessly. The neighbors said the Taylor woman was crazy and ought to be locked away. But Sloane, even at eight, knew they were wrong. Her mother was right about the voices; Sloane knew this because she, too, heard them.

Inevitably, her mother edged further and further toward insanity. When her mind finally snapped, it was a nightmare of terror for the little girl. For months after her mother had been hauled away by white-coated attendants, the young Sloane had relived the horror, hearing her mother shriek and cry, watching the medics wrestle her to the floor, seeing again the neighbors' avid expressions and hearing their cruel remarks. "Nutty as a fruit-cake . . ." "Always was somethin' strange about her . . ." "That youngun's a bit peculiar herself, if you ask me . . ." And later, after she'd been told by the elderly cousins who'd taken her in that her mother was dead by her own hand, Sloane had feared the same fate awaited her. Hadn't Cousin Oliver said so? "That child's just like her mother and her grandpa, cursed from birth. Sometimes she knows what I'm gonna say before I ever git the words out."

And Cousin Leitha had agreed: "It'd be best if the line died out with her, 'stead of passing it on to another innocent child." Not long afterward the cousins had left Sloane with the welfare depart-ment, unwilling to take responsibility for a little girl who was "touched by the hand of Satan."

This, then, was Sloane's legacy, the forces that had shaped her inner strength, defenses, and deter-mination to keep that kind of anguish and fear away from herself and those she loved. How would Santee feel if she slipped one day while all his lifelong friends and neighbors looked on in horror? Could he deal with the whispering and ostracism? Could an adopted child cope with the ugliness that would be inevitable if her secret ever became known? What right had she to even take the chance of ruining another person's life? She could foresee the problems, but not the solutions.

For the next few hours, Sloane had the house to herself except for Marcie, Hank's wife, a quiet and unobtrusive woman who helped Sloane shower, dress, and fix her hair. Then, with a shy smile, she excused herself to get back to her own household.

Santee's house was large and warm, with gracefully worn oak furniture, chintz curtains, a few antique pieces lovingly placed to show off their beauty. Large windows framed the view of the surrounding valley, admitting the peaceful serenity of the outdoors into the long den as well as into the upstairs bedrooms. On the walls and tables, photographs ranging from tintypes to Polaroids bespoke the heritage of the house and its family. She didn't imagine it had been changed much since Santee's mother was alive.

The kitchen, dominated by a huge table and ten chairs, was a chef's dream, filled with modern gadgets and appliances alongside an ancient black wood-burning stove, which now seemed to be used for storing pots and pans.

With the spacious rooms and hundreds of acres to explore, the ranch was an ideal place to raise "a passel of kids." The memory of his words overwhelmed her with depression.

Outside, she knew, Santee was going through his daily routine. More than anything she wished this were her kitchen, her man doing his chores, her arms he would come to each night. For just a moment, as she stared out at the frosty hills, she was on the verge of calling to him, telling him she had changed her mind. But she couldn't; it would be too unfair to both of them.

As she watched, Santee emerged from the barn and spoke with one of the hands, Jimbo, she thought, who gestured toward the front of the house. Santee's scowl was evident even from a distance. Curious, Sloane hurried through the formal dining room into the den to peer through the window.

A small white car was parked next to Santee's station wagon, and a man, out of place in a brown suit, stood looking at the outbuildings.

Michael! What would happen when he and Santee met? She didn't have long to wait to find out.

Santee strode into sight, defiance and rage in every step. She could almost hear his voice, low and menacing, as he obviously ordered Michael off the ranch. Michael shook his head, speaking quickly for a moment. When Santee stepped forward with a threatening gesture, she stumbled to the front door and threw it open.

"Santee!"

He stopped in midswing. "Get back in the house, Sloane!"

"Sloane, you shouldn't be out here," Michael echoed.

"Michael, what are you doing here?" Dizziness swept over her, and she braced herself on the porch railing with her good hand. "You didn't tell me you were coming."

206

"When I heard you were injured, I had to see for myself that you were all right."

Santee hadn't missed her unsteadiness, the slight breathiness in her voice. "Get out of the way, Fielding," he growled, pushing Michael aside in his haste.

He swung Sloane up into his arms and carried her into the den, where he laid her on the long sofa. "What the hell were you doing outside? You should be in bed."

Her gaze went past his shoulder to Michael, who had followed them inside and now stood, ill at ease, in the doorway. "Sloane, are you all right?"

Santee turned a black look on him. "I thought I told you to get off my land, Fielding. If you hurry you can still make it under your own steam."

Looking at Sloane with a questioning glance, Michael asked, "Who is this man? Not a friend of yours, I hope."

Sloane glared at her ex-husband. "This is Lucas Santee, Michael. If you get the feeling he'd like to murder you, you're right. Rena Davidson was his sister."

Michael paled. "I won't bother telling you how sorry I am, Mr. Santee. I don't think you'd believe me. Sloane, I've come a long way to see you. Could we go somewhere and talk?"

"She's not leaving this ranch. Say what you came to say, and get out!"

"Santee, please," she pleaded. "I know what

you're feeling. But let me handle it. After all, he has helped . . ."

"He helped Rena to die. He helped you to take the blame. And if he's not off this ranch in five minutes, he'll need some help of his own." With that, he left the room, but Sloane noticed he didn't go farther than the kitchen, within easy earshot.

Pulling up a chair, Michael sat close to her, touching her shoulder.

"Sloane, I want you to leave here with me. You and I both know Chapman's somewhere nearby, just waiting for his chance. You're not safe here. Please come back to Dallas with me, where I can protect you."

"Michael, you never cease to amaze me," she said wearily. "It hasn't been that long ago that you were calling me names, telling me you never wanted to see me again. In fact, you paid rather generously to get me out of your life. This all seems to be a little out of character for you."

He looked pained. As Sloane remembered, that was one of Michael's favorite looks, being so often practiced.

"Darling, believe me, I'd die myself if it would bring Rena back and change what happened three years ago. I was a different person then, someone I didn't like very well, even at the time. But I've changed, Sloane, I've really changed. These three years have been hell for me. Please, let me try to make it up to you."

He grabbed her hand, squeezing it tightly, and

in that moment she had a flash, not much more than a nudge but strong enough to convince her he was telling the truth as he knew it. She also realized his greatest need was to ease his conscience, not to comfort her. Michael had lost his greatest asset, his self-image, and now he was riddled with guilt and shame.

"All right, Fielding, your time's up. Get out." Santee had approached silently and now stood glaring at Sloane's ex-husband.

"Not without Sloane."

"She's not going anywhere with you . . ."

"Santee," she interrupted, "I can make my own decisions. In fact, I'd like Michael to take me home—back to my cabin," she added, squelching the flicker of hope she'd seen in Michael's eyes. "He can stay with me a day or two, until I can get around better. Then I'll go into Denver and stay with Carol."

Even as she said the words, she hated herself for the pain she was inflicting on the man she loved. But it was a solution. He'd be angry enough now to let her go, and she had to get away. Another few days with him and she wouldn't have the strength to leave.

His face closed against her, but she caught the bellow of pain from his mind. He left the room without speaking.

"Michael, would you wait in the car for me? I have a few things to gather up, then I'll be out."

"Are you sure?" He glanced warily over his

shoulder. "Maybe I should stay here and help you with your things."

"No." There would be no reasoning with Santee now. "I'll be all right."

When she had packed her few toiletries, she went to Santee's study. He was looking out the window at Mt. Evans, his back stiff with anger.

"Goodbye, Santee."

He didn't face her when he answered. "I know what you're doing, Sloane, and why. Right now I could almost hate you for it. Not because you're leaving with him, but because you didn't have the guts to stay."

There was nothing she could say. She left, closing the door softly behind her.

As was to be expected, Michael was a model house guest. He didn't make messes, he was very solicitous of her needs, and he even did most of the cooking. What was surprising was his reticence. Only once, his first night in the cabin, did he attempt to change her mind.

"Darling, at least consider coming back to Dallas. You could set the terms—maybe a trial period. I'd make no demands on you; all I ask is a chance to regain your confidence."

"This is pointless," she'd answered firmly. "I have no intention of going back to you. I've tried not to hate you, and I think I've succeeded. And I appreciate all you've done these past few weeks. But I haven't forgiven you; I can't. I'm tired now.

I'd like to go to bed.'' She sensed something like relief in his expression, as though he could now say to himself: *I've done all I can; now I'm off the hook.*

She was halfway up the stairs when he spoke again. ''Sloane, who is Santee? I mean, what is he to you?''

''He's the man I love.''

The next day, neither of them mentioned what had been said the night before. He asked about her career and listened attentively to her plans for the art exhibit. But soon he was, as usual, talking about himself. Since retiring from the political circus, he told her, he had resumed his private law practice and was doing quite well. His new offices were in a choice location in the latest office complex on the LBJ Freeway, his clients some of the most influential citizens in Texas, his secretary the most efficient. . . .

By midafternoon she was almost grateful for the pounding headache that gave her an excuse to escape to the peace of her bedroom.

She took one of the tablets the doctor had prescribed, and within minutes, she had dozed off. Once she roused, thinking she had heard the telephone, but when it didn't ring again, she went back to sleep immediately.

''This is Sheriff Lambert. I'd like to speak to Miss Taylor.''

''Yes, Sheriff. Michael Fielding here. Sloane is resting now. I'd be glad to take a message.''

"Well, it's kind of important. One of my deputies picked up a guy who looks a lot like the telefax photo we have of Chapman. All we've got on him is a vagrancy charge, so we can't hold him for long. I was hoping Miss Taylor could make a positive I.D."

"There's no need to bother her, Sheriff. I can identify Chapman. I'll be at your office in half an hour."

Santee drove the pickup into Ernie Crow's station, slamming the door when he got out. He was still in a rare mood, had been ever since he watched Fielding drive Sloane down the narrow road off the ranch. Torn between anger at her lack of spirit and compassion for the emotional trauma he knew she'd suffered, he couldn't decide whether to call her, go see her, or try to forget her. He half-suspected this trip into town was a subconscious excuse to cut the distance between them by half. From here, it was only a few more miles out to her place. . . .

"How's it goin', Luke? You need a fill-up today?"

"Yeah, Ernie, just put it on my bill. Have you seen Will Lambert around today?"

"Naw, guess he's stayin' purty busy in the office. One of his depitties brought a feller in a little while ago. By the way, how's Miz Taylor gittin' along? Heard she was stayin' at yore place 'til she's up and around."

"She's coming along fine, Ernie. Just a few bumps and bruises."

"Reckon that feller wuz wantin' directions to her place didn't find her, then, her bein' in the hospital and all, then out at Crooked Creek."

"Yeah, he found her. Drove out to the ranch yesterday."

"Wuddent the same guy, then. I b'lieve this one musta been hitchhikin', leastways ridin' with somebody. Heard him tell the driver to just drop him at the end of the road."

"This wasn't yesterday?" Sudden alarm gripped his stomach. "A man in a white sedan?"

"Naw, a coupla days ago, in a old red Buick."

Santee jerked the nozzle from the gas tank and was in front of Lambert's office within thirty seconds. He didn't miss the white car in the next space.

"God damn it, Fielding, where's Sloane?" he shouted, crashing the door against the wall.

Startled, both Michael and Lambert jerked around to face him.

"She's at home . . ."

"Lucas, what's going on?"

"Ernie Crow just told me somebody asked directions to Sloane's place two days ago, a hitchhiker. It has to be Chapman!"

"Son of a bitch!" Lambert stared in consternation. "We thought we had him, Lucas, but Mr. Fielding just told us we got the wrong guy."

Before he could blink, Michael was flying backward to land with a thud against the wall. "If she's hurt because of your stupidity, Fielding, you're a dead man! Will, see if you can get her on the phone, then follow me out there."

The knife sliced through the telephone wire cleanly. This was the break he'd been waiting for. She had the cabin pretty well secured, but she hadn't pulled the bars across the deck door since she unlocked them this morning.

Funny how Fielding had rushed off like that. But it was easier this way. He'd planned to make his move just after dark anyway and take care of Fielding, too, if necessary. That cave on the other side of the hill was cold, and he'd be glad to see the last of it.

There was an important telephone call, her dream self said, *but it wasn't coming through.* She kept lifting the receiver, over and over, but there was only dead silence on the other end. But she kept trying, because it was so important. It had something to do with the man standing in the trees, the man who was holding the knife. And somewhere Santee was calling her, *Sloane, I'm coming, sweetheart; I'm on my way, just hold on.*

Then she put it all together. She knew what was happening, but she couldn't quite wake up, but she had to, she had to, he was here, Chapman was here, he was right outside, oh, God, get up, Sloane, get up. . . .

The security bars! She lunged out of bed, fell against the folding iron gate, shoved it into place, heard it click. Through the bars she saw Chapman lift himself over the deck railing, saw his face distorted with rage.

He threw himself against the heavy glass, beating on it with his fist. In his other hand he held a knife, the cutting edge reflecting the afternoon sunlight. She backed away, her throat ripping apart with the force of her screams.

Santee leapt from the cab of the truck and raced to the front door. From inside he could hear her screaming while he pounded futilely. Chapman couldn't have gotten in this way, he realized, and ran for the back of the cabin. The unmelted snow in the cabin's shadow was disturbed, the footprints blatantly clear. They stopped directly under the deck. It would have been easy for a man to catch one of the exposed timbers and pull himself up. He had to get in, he had to protect her.

A sudden movement, a furtive sound were his only warnings. He had no time to dodge the body that landed on his back, twisting and fighting. He flipped the weight off and whirled, meeting another attack. The man was strong, very strong; and as they struggled, he cursed steadily, obscenely. Santee smashed a huge fist into Chapman's face and knew a surge of pleasure at the sound of breaking cartilage. A sudden sear of pain burned into his shoulder, but he ignored it and concentrated instead on trying to wrestle Chapman to the ground.

The bastard knew how to fight, Santee acknowledged, and he'd obviously learned it all in a tough school. Kicking, gouging, slashing, the two combatants methodically tried to destroy one another. More than once Santee felt the tug as the deadly blade sliced through the lined sheepskin of his coat. His wound had blazed into a consuming pain, and he felt himself weakening. Chapman's sudden thrust sent him heavily to the ground. He recovered instantly and dove at his enemy, but his arms closed on empty air.

Behind him, Lambert shouted, "Get down, Lucas!" He hit the ground and a report rang out. Close by there was a grunt of pain. Santee saw Chapman stagger and fall, then regain his footing and turn for the trees. Santee launched himself at the fleeing man, but a heavy fist, hard as iron, clubbed him down. Another shot narrowly missed Chapman. In one last desperate move, Chapman lifted a small log and hurled it at the sheriff; the improvised missile glanced off Lambert's shoulder, knocking the gun out of his hand.

To both the watching men, Chapman seemed to disappear into the trees like a wraith.

Then Will was helping Santee to his feet. "I hit him, Lucas; I swear I did, but he didn't even slow down. You see to Sloane, I'm going after him."

Walking in slow motion, Sloane finally made it to the door, unlocked it, and opened it to Santee.

Her eyes were huge in her white face, and all she could see was the bloodstain spreading across his chest where his coat had been ripped away.

The building pressure exploded in her ears, and she crumpled to the floor.

Chapter Eleven

THIS WAS HER night. Glitter, glamour, acclaim, recognition—they were all just around the corner, according to Carol and van Buren. The mirror told her she certainly looked the part. An off-the-shoulder black dress, classically simple, lent her an air of quiet elegance; her hair was pulled back and fastened high on each side with sparkling clips that matched her small drop earrings and pendant.

Carol had helped her apply makeup with a masterful hand, and now she could almost believe the tall beauty reflected in the mirror wasn't Sloane Taylor at all, but a polished, sophisticated imposter.

Seven o'clock. In one hour, she would walk into a crowded art gallery, smile and mingle, talk shop, shake hands, listen to endless gossip and chatter—and hope no one could see the emptiness behind her eyes.

Only Carol knew what she'd been through these past two weeks. More than once during that time the two women had talked late into the night, Sloane spilling out all her fear, heartache, and despair onto Carol's loving shoulders. She sometimes thought if it weren't for Carol's steady friendship, she wouldn't have made it through with her sanity intact. At odd moments during the day, when she was polishing up a piece or watching TV or washing her hair, Chapman's face would suddenly loom before her, twisted with insane hatred and rage as she had last seen it. Or she would see again the ugly spread of blood across Santee's shirt, reliving the split second before she had fainted when she thought he was fatally wounded and knew it was her fault. Because of her, Chapman was in Colorado; because of her, Santee had come to the cabin that day; because of her, he had been stabbed.

Later everyone—including Santee—had reassured her his wound was only superficial, but the horror of what had nearly happened would not abate. Now more than ever she had reason to stay out of his life, and she clung to her resolve. She had neither seen nor spoken to him in two weeks. As long as Chapman was alive and free, neither Sloane nor anyone close to her was safe.

So far, because of the insistence of both Will

Lambert and Carol, she had stayed in Denver with her friend. The city was an anonymous place, they all insisted; and everyone in Snowcrest believed she had just packed up and moved, forwarding address unknown. It had taken about five minutes for that carefully planted rumor to get around town, Will had joked, so even if Chapman recovered from the bullet he had taken, there were no more leads for him to follow. For all practical purposes, Sloane Taylor had disappeared.

Even the art exhibit hadn't been publicized; instead, private invitations had been sent to over 200 of the gallery's clients and patrons. Everything possible had been done to ensure her safety, but still she was constantly on edge. Late nights, early mornings, and lots of hard work and concentration—that seemed to be the sum total of her existence these days.

"Are you ready? It's nearly time," Carol announced. "Wow! You look terrific, sweetie. If I didn't love you, I'd be jealous as hell."

"Why? If you think anyone will be looking at me after you walk in, you'd better think again. Red is definitely your color. I'd give anything if I had the nerve to wear a dress like that."

Which wasn't precisely true. Nerve wasn't enough to carry off that costume. It took flair, which Carol had in abundance. Backless, skintight, cherry red, and slit from ankle to thigh, it was one of the most daring dresses she'd ever seen. And, of course, it was perfect for Carol.

"Well, as someone once said, if you got it, flaunt it. Which I fully intend to do." She glanced in the mirror to check her makeup. "By the way, Lucas called again," she said, too casually.

Sloane concentrated on fastening the clasp of her full-length gray satin cape. "What did he want?"

"What does he always want? To find out how you are, to talk to you, to see you." Obviously aggravated with her friend, Carol's voice rose an octave. "The least you could do . . ."

"Don't use that tone with me," Sloane snapped. "You know my reasons and you know I'm right." She snatched her bag from the dresser and flounced out the door into the living room.

"I'm sorry, honey," Carol placated from close behind. "I know you believe this is best for both of you. But you're wrong. This—problem—could work itself out if you'd just give it a chance. And Chapman won't be on the loose forever. He may already be dead."

"Carol, don't do this to me. I really can't stand any more. I'm leaving now, if you'd like to go with me. Otherwise, I'll take a cab."

On the way to the gallery, Carol tried to restrict herself to less controversial topics, recognizing Sloane's tenuous grip on emotional stability. Now that she knew the whole story, Carol thought Sloane's strength of character nothing short of miraculous. How she had dealt with Chapman, not to mention that weird mind-reading trip, was beyond

Carol's comprehension. And now things had been further complicated by Santee. Personally, Carol couldn't see that the problems were all that insurmountable, but it was what Sloane believed that mattered. The strain Sloane was under was unbearable, and it broke Carol's heart to see what was happening.

"Have you talked to Will lately?" she asked, when the silence had grown uncomfortable.

"This morning," Sloane replied. "There's been nothing on Chapman, but they're still looking."

"I don't understand how he could just disappear like that. I mean, the man was *shot*, he bled like crazy, then—poof! Nothing. He has to be on that mountain somewhere."

Sloane smiled mockingly. "You don't know him. He's not dead, and he's not gone. He'll be back."

"Creepy," Carol shuddered. "You don't think he would have headed for home, back to Dallas?"

"Not if he thinks I'm still here."

"Oh, Miss Taylor—may I call you Sloane?—I can't tell you how much I've looked forward to meeting you! Your work is just magnificent, so fresh and open." The pleasant-faced lady with blue hair beamed at the object of her praise and patted her shoulder approvingly. "I think you have a great future, dear."

Sloane smiled and thanked her, moved on to the

next group of well-dressed, slightly tipsy people where she accepted compliments, fielded passes, and graciously refused countless invitations to cocktail parties and intimate dinners ("just a few close friends"). It had been like this all night and she was exhausted, not to mention a bit tipsy herself. The champagne cocktails were flowing freely and she'd enjoyed all four of hers immensely.

She rarely drank, and after getting soused with Carol she'd vowed to never again bend an elbow in public. But as the night wore on, she found herself having one sip after another until finally Mr. van Buren himself commented on it.

"Young lady, I hope you're not going to disgrace me tonight after I've been so thoroughly complimented on my good taste in having found you." He was resplendent in his finery, a most handsome man, Sloane decided, peering at him closely.

"Oh, no, I don't think so," she replied. "I'm hardly ever disgraceful."

"Yes, well, I think we'll postpone the interview that young man has been angling for. I'd feel more comfortable if you waited until you knew what you were saying."

She saluted. "Yes sir. I bow to your superior wisdom."

As she began her bow, he hastily stopped her. "Never mind, Sloane, I get your drift." He patted her shoulder and grimaced in a thin-lipped, cool manner that passed for a smile. "At least you're not a maudlin drunk, thank God."

She waved at his departing back, then stopped a waiter who was threading his way through the maze of guests and lifted a fresh glass from his tray. A light touch on her back surprised her into spilling half the drink on the floor.

"If you can't handle it, better put it away," drawled a familiar, achingly precious voice.

She whirled and found herself facing his smile.

"You're incredibly lovely, Sloane."

"I—I didn't know you were coming," she managed weakly. He was so beautiful! More than anything she wanted to touch him.

"Did you really think Carol would leave me off the guest list? Besides, I have to dress up every ten years or so, just to see if I still know how."

"I'd say you have it down pat. I mean, your buttons are straight and everything." She couldn't tell him what she really thought, how wonderful he looked, how wonderful he would look no matter what he wore. But tonight, completely at ease in a black tuxedo, he was so far removed from his usual appearance she felt as if she were looking at a different man. *But then,* she reminded herself, *you thought the same thing when you looked in the mirror.* Maybe the clothes had somehow magically transformed them into different people, fantasy characters who lived only on the pages of a romance novel with no tragedies to haunt them.

He stepped closer to her; she could feel his breath. "I've missed you."

"Don't," she murmured. "I wish you hadn't come."

"Liar, I saw it in your eyes when you turned around. You were glad to see me. If I took you in my arms right here and kissed you the way I want to, you'd kiss me back."

She couldn't tell whether he was smiling or smirking; probably the latter, but she didn't have enough energy for indignation. Besides, at the moment he was making a lot of sense.

"Why are you doing this to me?"

"Doing what, sweet Sloane?" He was closer than ever, setting her pulses pounding. The champagne was doing strange things to her head; she was having difficulty remembering just why she'd left him in the first place. It was hard to think when everything was spinning past her . . .

"What's wrong?" He caught her arm as she swayed, guided her to a long sofa against the wall. "Can I bring you something? Is it your head?"

Through the crowd, Carol had seen them and hurried to investigate, leaving her latest conquest to stare after her in puzzlement. "Are you two fighting again? What's going on? Sloane, you don't look well, you're white as a sheet!"

With Santee and Carol towering over her, the situation suddenly seemed most amusing to Sloane who, from her vantage point, could now see things ever so much more clearly. She giggled. "You look just like Barbie and Ken, except Barbie has bigger—well, you know—and her hair's longer, too."

Santee blinked, then his great laugh burst out and filled the room, while Carol was at a loss for words, a rare event in her life.

"She's smashed!" Santee explained, still grinning. "Probably for the first time in her life."

"The second," volunteered Carol. "I should have remembered, she doesn't have a good head for wine."

"Bless you. This makes things a lot easier."

Now his smile was definitely a smirk, but Sloane was past caring, even when he grasped her elbow and hauled her to her feet. "Carol, would you get her coat?" he said, steadying his somewhat woozy charge.

"Lucas Santee, what are you doing?" Carol gasped.

"I'm just going to drive the lady home, like the gentleman I am."

She couldn't resist the gleam in his eye and smiled her approval. Trust Santee to get to the heart of the matter, she thought. "You'd better take this, then," she said, offering him her own cocktail, "just in case she starts sobering up."

Sloane slept during most of the trip to Crooked Creek, woke only once to ask where they were going, then dropped off again without waiting for an answer. And when he lifted her from the front seat to carry her gently into the house, she merely sighed and wrapped her arms around his neck. Even in his bedroom, while he carefully undressed her, she made no protest.

For what was left of the night, Santee held her close, content with the softness of her skin and the smell of her hair. He knew he was taking a chance; when she woke, she might hate him for what was tantamount to kidnapping, but he was sick and tired of humoring her and understanding her—and missing her. He'd always had the feeling that if only he could hold her long enough, the magic between them would break down all the barriers. Finally he had the chance to find out if he was right.

Dawn was just breaking when she opened her eyes. For a moment she stared at him blankly, then when realization struck her she tried to push him way, tears streaming down her face. "This isn't fair, Santee!"

"I never said I'd be fair, darlin'. I just said I wouldn't give up, remember? If this is the only way to convince you I'm right, then this is the way it'll be."

First he kissed away the salty drops that wet her cheeks, then he moved on to her eyelids, her temples, down to her neck. His lips were soft, coaxing, persuasive, and they drew from her the

only response she was capable of giving him—
total surrender.

They compromised. She agreed to stay a week
if, at the end of that time, he promised to let go if
she thought it wasn't working. It was weakness,
she knew, to give in. But she couldn't seem to
think straight anymore. It was like a drug in her
system, this need for him. His voice calmed her,
his touch excited her, his love completed her. If
she'd had an ounce of willpower, she fumed silently, she'd have left his bed and walked back to
town.

But she hadn't, and now it was too late. Every
day, every hour that went by was so close to
perfect she could find no excuse for leaving. They
never quarreled, except about politics, and that
was allowed, he told her gravely. Every couple
should have one area in which they could indulge
in open hostilities, then the rest of the relationship
could remain a Demilitarized Zone. Just as gravely,
she agreed.

And no matter what they did together, it was
fun. She had just as soon muck out the stables as
go to a fancy restaurant for her favorite meal, as
long as she was with him. They did both and much
more.

After five days, she caught herself telling him
about her plans to redecorate the den and stopped
abruptly in midsentence.

"See there?" he whispered into her ear. "See how easy it was when you stopped fighting it, love?"

She was miserable. "Nothing's changed, though. All the reasons I had for not wanting this are still there. Don't you understand? I'm so happy with you, and I *know* it can't last!"

"It'll last, Sloane. And the reasons *have* changed, because I've proved you wrong." He kissed her, his eyes tender and full of love.

"What are you talking about? The only thing you've proved is that I can't say no to you."

He grinned and pulled her down to sit on his lap. "Do you remember me telling you about the time I spent in the Army, when my buddy was killed in that training accident?"

"Yes. It was terrible. You said you'd never told anyone before."

He nodded. He was going to drop a bomb on her; she could feel it coming. "I never could talk about it before; it was one of those things too painful to share. And do you remember us talking about my father's death and the way I was afraid to love anybody, because I thought if I loved them, they would die?"

She was more and more bemused. "But what does that have to do with me being wrong and you being right?"

"Because, sweetheart, I didn't really tell you those things." He paused, watching her face closely.

"You've been carrying on one-sided conversations with me all week."

At first the words didn't register; then, gradually, she understood. The blood drained from her face and she felt sick. "And I didn't even realize," she whispered. "I told you it would happen."

He pressed her more tightly against his lap as she struggled to get up. "Yes, it happened. And guess what? It's okay, honey. I don't feel violated or betrayed or anything except loved. It's—surprising when it happens, and it'll take some getting used to. But it sure cuts down on conversation."

Looking into his eyes, she felt everything he was trying to say: that he needed her like the earth needs water. And that if she left him, he'd miss her for the rest of his life. And that he'd always be there to remind her that being different wasn't so bad, if you had someone to share it with.

They sat up until the next morning, making plans and making love. Neither one of them mentioned Chapman.

She was finally here. He knew she'd show up sooner or later, just like he knew it would be Santee she'd come to. That wasn't hard to figure out, the way he'd come running that day. It had been harder to find out who Santee was, but he'd managed. Good thing he'd decided to watch her cabin one more day or he'd have missed seeing Santee load up her things. That bullet in the arm had kept him holed up so long, he had started to worry that she'd slipped past him.

Yessir, he sure had a lot to be grateful to Santee for; first, for providing him with this fine place to stay. Nothing much but a shack, but it kept the wind off; and the nearby deadfall provided easy pickings for the fireplace, even though he could only use it for a few hours each night when he was sure no one would see the smoke.

Mostly, though, he was grateful to the rancher for bringing her right out here to him.

He'd remember to express his gratitude before he left.

Chapter Twelve

". . . THE IMPORTANT THING is that you're happy, Sloane. I wish you all the best," Michael was saying when Santee teasingly put his head next to hers, sandwiching the receiver between their ears.

"It was nice hearing from you, Michael. Thank you for calling," she replied, gasping when Santee yanked the receiver from her hand to add his own personal message.

"Yes, indeed, Michael. Thank you so much and goodbye." With that he none too gently hung up the phone.

"Well, I guess you told him, huh?" she teased. "Feel better?"

"Immensely. The only thing I'd enjoy more is hitting him again."

She giggled. "I still can't believe you did that! Will told Carol he was out for nearly five minutes."

"Is that all? And that was my best punch." He wrapped his arms around her waist and lifted her to meet his kiss. "Now bundle up, we've got some ground to cover."

He waited while she went to the bedroom to change into boots. The room with its huge bed was now familiar and comfortable. Sometimes she found it hard to believe she'd been here such a short time, so firmly entrenched had she become in Santee's life. The doubts still crept in at odd moments, of course; they had been the basis for her actions most of her life and she hadn't expected to shed them quickly or easily. But with every day that passed, they faded more and more. Maybe too much so, she thought, suddenly nervous. Maybe they were too happy, she and Santee, too confident and secure. What if it wasn't yet over?

Nonsense, she answered herself. True, Chapman hadn't been found. But the country had been scoured for a radius of twenty miles, and all the clues pointed to the wounded fugitive having slipped past the search parties. A motorist had reported picking up a hitchhiker matching Chapman's description, a man who seemed ill or injured; the driver had dropped his passenger off at Raton Pass, near the New Mexico border. Still, they couldn't be *positive*.

She gave herself a mental shake and forced her mind to happier thoughts. Grabbing a coat from the closet, she rejoined Santee in the living room. Then, arms entwined, they walked to the barn.

The horses were saddled and waiting, Hank holding the reins while Sloane mounted up. It had been years since she'd been riding, and it felt awkward at first, but she knew it wouldn't take long for the technique to come back to her. She had been looking forward to this ever since yesterday when Santee had promised her a complete tour of the ranch on horseback.

"We'll be back by sundown," Santee told Hank. "If the vet calls, tell him I'd like him to stop by and take a look at Cinnamon first chance he gets."

"Sure thing, boss. Have a nice ride."

The weather couldn't have been more perfect for November—just chilly enough to be invigorating, with sunlight to warm their backs and no wind to chap their skins.

"Come on, cowboy, let's get this herd on the trail," she called over her shoulder as she urged her mount to a canter, leaving Santee behind to close the gate.

He overtook her effortlessly, and they began to range the hills, valleys, pastures, and timberland that comprised Crooked Creek.

"See that tree?" Santee pointed out a spruce growing at an odd angle. About two feet from the ground, the trunk made an abrupt ninety-degree turn. "When I was about seven, I heard my father say 'as the twig is bent, so grows the tree.' So I tried it."

"Well, it worked," she laughed. "What else did you mutilate?"

"That wasn't mutilation!" he protested. "That was a gin-you-wine scientific experiment!"

"I'll bet. You were probably a rotten kid, Lucas Santee. You still have a dangerous gleam in your eye."

"Well, I have to admit to a few pranks, but nothing lethal. And of course I'm completely harmless now. My vices are restricted to lusting after beautiful women."

The gleam she had mentioned turned upon her with full force. If heaven really existed, she thought, it would be like this, an eternity of laughing and loving with Santee.

"Would you like to stop and lust for a while?" she offered.

He shook his head. "Not here. There's a much better spot over that rise. It's where I seduce all my women."

"Well, from now on it's got a 'restricted' sign on it," she retorted, urging the mare forward.

The whole afternoon went that way, easy and peaceful and filled with laughter. They talked about their pasts with an ease born of true intimacy and trust; they planned their future with a hope born of love. About three o'clock, they stopped by the stream that cut across the ranch from east to west and picnicked on the ham sandwiches Salty had packed for them. He'd even packed linen napkins in the saddlebags along with the food.

"Your influence is showing already," Santee teased her. "Salty said, and I quote, 'It's about time we showed a little class around here.' "

The picnic over, they remounted to continue their unhurried, rambling ride, Santee pointing out each of his favorite childhood playgrounds and telling stories of his parents and some of his boyish escapades.

"Over there is the world's most heavily traveled ambush route," he told her, indicating an isolated clump of cedar. "Every Saturday us good guys rode through there on our way to save the fort, and every time the bad guys jumped out and surrounded us. Of course, we took turns winning. We were very heavy on democracy."

A chill blew across the back of her neck and she shivered. The flash was disconcerting but so brief and unclear she couldn't isolate it or even be absolutely sure it had happened. Trying to attribute the incident to nervous pessimism, she decided to ignore it, turning up her coat collar and concentrating on Santee's words.

He had noticed the gesture, however, and reined up reluctantly. "We'd better start back, honey. It gets dark pretty early, and the wind's coming up. I don't want you to overdo your first time out."

"Already? I wanted to ride up the mountain, and we haven't been to the old homestead yet."

"And I wanted you to see the deadfall where I used to play 'fort.' But we'll have to make it next time, and we'll start earlier so you can see everything.'' He edged his mount closer to hers, then leaned in the saddle to kiss her lightly. ''We've got all the time in the world, sweetheart.''

She accepted his verdict with a smile, supremely happy.

On the way back, they rode close to the timberline to check for any breaks in the fence. Santee explained how difficult it was to find livestock once it got through to the heavily wooded areas.

''The homestead cabin is right through there,'' he told her when they paused at the crest of a small hill, ''about a hundred yards beyond the fence . . .'' He stopped speaking abruptly and turned to peer into the trees.

''What is it?''

''Thought I heard something. Maybe a deer.''

Then she heard it, too—something rustling through the undergrowth.

He dismounted. ''Wait here while I check. Could be some stock strayed from the next ranch.''

Without warning, tension knotted the muscles at the base of her skull and her flesh crawled. ''Don't go in there, Santee.''

Her voice sounded strained and harsh even to her own ears; he looked at her closely, eyes narrowed. ''What's wrong?''

''I don't know. Just please don't go in there,'' she pleaded, fighting the urge to kick her horse into a gallop. ''Let's go back to the ranch. Now. Please.''

He didn't question her further, but put his boot

in the stirrup. As he turned, something flew from out of the trees, hitting the gelding hard on the flank. The horse reared and whinnied, throwing Santee to the ground in its frenzy to bolt.

Startled, Sloane's mare began to prance as she cried out. "What happened? Santee, are you all right?" She slid from the saddle and ran toward him.

"Don't!" he shouted. "Get out of here!"

"What . . . ?"

Then her horse, too, was gone, rolling its eyes in terror.

She felt him then, when it was too late. Like a magnet, his unseen presence drew her eyes to the thick timber where a man could crouch in the semidarkness and throw sharp stones at the horses. She knelt beside Santee. "He's here," she said quietly. "I can feel him."

His face hardened. "It's three miles back to the ranch. And my rifle just took off with the horse." He tried to stand and grimaced. "Damn! My knee hit a rock when I fell."

Shock and sudden terror sharpened her senses. She felt the flow beginning but was unable to block it. From somewhere outside herself, she observed the scene dispassionately, watching the other Sloane report what was happening inside her head.

"He's wondering if you're hurt. He's hoping you are."

Santee heard the unnatural calm in her voice and

his heart skipped a beat. "Honey, listen to me. We're going to be all right. But you have to help me." Roughly he shook her when she didn't respond. "Listen, Sloane! I can't do it without you. Do you hear me?"

Her eyes focused on him then, as if he had called her back from a faraway land. "Yes. I'm all right now, I promise." A shudder rippled over her as fear set in with a vengeance. "What do you want me to do?"

"You just said you could hear him. Is he still there?"

"Yes, but I can't tell where." She didn't want to know where and couldn't understand Santee's sudden intensity until he spoke again.

"Do you think you can stay with him, tell me what he's planning?"

Wide-eyed with comprehension, she nodded. "Maybe. He's—jumbled—a lot of the time. But I'll try." *And I'll do it. This time I'll make this damned curse work for me.*

"Okay." He hugged her. "In a few minutes it'll be dark, then we'll make it to the gully. It's about a hundred yards east. Once we get down into it, we'll move south. That'll bring us out near the back pasture. Understand?"

She nodded, darting her eyes nervously toward the woods. "He's moving closer now. He can't see us clearly in the dark, but he doesn't want us to see him yet." She paused to sort out the confused images. "If he can get close enough, he'll go for you first. He figures you must be hurt or we'd have done something by now.'' The uncanny clarity of Chapman's thoughts was unnerving, and she tried to block out her fear.

"He's got that right.'' Gritting his teeth against the pain, he heaved himself up on his good leg. "Honey, I'm hurt worse than I thought. Maybe you should try to get back to the house on your own.''

"I won't leave without you.'' Santee needed her. He still underestimated Chapman. But she didn't; she knew she was their only hope for survival.

"But you can travel faster than I can, go on ahead for help.''

"You need me to stay one jump ahead of him. We stay together.''

He accepted her decision without further argument. "You're quite a lady.''

She reached for his hand, squeezed it. "I think we'd better go. Since you stood up, he's not so sure you're hurt. And he's angry because it's so dark.''

"Good. Angry men make mistakes.'' Santee grunted with the effort of trying to walk without a limp, while she willed herself not to help him, to walk naturally; and all the time he talked to her softly, as though gentling a skittish horse.

"The ground's kind of uneven right through here, honey, so take it easy. And be careful climbing down into the gully. It's steep and rough.''

It took forever to walk the distance, and she found herself counting the steps. Sixty-five . . . sixty-six . . . sixty-seven . . .

Then they were there, sliding down the bare earth on their backsides. For several more minutes, they walked in silence, touching one another for reassurance.

"He's decided to come out of the trees." Sweat popped out on her forehead, feeling clammy in the cold night air. Mentally she was exhausted from coping with the obscenity of his derangement, but she couldn't let Santee know. Her psi ability was the only weapon they had, and she would ply it with all the strength at her command. "He's afraid he's lost us . . . he's climbing over the fence . . ."

Santee's breathing was labored and he stumbled often, but he kept up the pace. *I should never have brought her out here. I was supposed to protect her, keep her safe . . .*

"It's nobody's fault, Santee. It would have happened sooner or later, here or somewhere else. As long as he's alive, it'll never be over." Neither of them remarked on what she had just done, but Santee worried that if she was receiving both him and Chapman it could wear her down too quickly. He concentrated on walking, on the pain in his knee, on next month's auction—anything that wouldn't distress her further.

Five minutes later they stopped to rest.

"He fell." Chapman was as weary as they were,

but with an added advantage—he was too crazy to care.

"I didn't hear anything. He must not be too close."

"I can't tell. He's loud but not very clear. . . . He's gone! I've lost him!" She clutched his arm desperately, tensed against the sudden rush, the searing pain of the blade, the unseen blow.

"Hush, it'll be okay." He hugged her tightly against his chest. "You'll get it back. Let's keep moving. We're about halfway there."

The seconds dragged by. Sloane thought she had never been so tired nor felt so hopeless. It had been completely dark for a long time. If she looked up, she could see the stars clearly, but in the gully, which rose a good three feet above their heads, the air seemed thick and heavy. Step and step and step, stumble, step and step . . .

She caught the flash an instant too late. The rock, thrown with herculean force from directly above her, hit her shoulder, sending shock waves of pain tearing through her body.

Someone yelled, maybe it was her, then she heard only the grunts of the two men grappling in the dark, the thuds of fists against flesh.

"Sloane, run! Get out of here!"

But she couldn't move. Her head swam and she fought down nausea. What could she do to help with only one good arm? *Two cripples against a madman with a knife.*

The blows continued, punctuated with Chapman's curses. A vague thought flitted across her consciousness—fistfights weren't Chapman's usual style. Any second she expected a sudden silence, a dreadful quiet signaling that Chapman's knife had once more found its mark. Nearly frantic with the need to help Santee, to save him, she almost missed the clue when it came again. Then a surge of joy coursed through her.

The knife! "Santee, he's lost the knife! He dropped it when he fell!" Elation, hope buoyed her up. They were even; they had a chance!

She found her footing and ran forward, stumbling into the two struggling men. Her mind fought for balance; she was reading both of them, reeling under the impact of the bloodlust each of them felt. Blindly she thrust out her hand, touched a shoulder, knew it was her enemy—she attacked, the throbbing of her injured shoulder forgotten. Her nails found his eyes and he screamed, flailing wildly to dislodge the wildcat on his back. With a mighty heave, he tossed her several feet into the air and she landed solidly on her back.

Winded, exhausted, desperate, she rose to her feet, trying to regain her senses before she joined the battle yet again. They were there, just ahead of her, she could hear them shouting. No, not them; it was someone else! She scrambled out of the gully, her body shrieking with the effort, and ran toward the flashlight beams. "Here, over here! Hurry!"

Strong arms caught her up as she fell, while

booted feet pounded past her to disappear down the steep embankment.

"There! Toward the trees!"

There was more shouting, more commotion, then several shots.

An incredulous roar of rage, a final disbelieving protest, filled her mind. Then Chapman blinked out, irrevocably silenced.

Epilogue

THERE WAS NOTHING quite as sweet-smelling as summer grass, she thought lazily, rolling over to turn her face up to the July sun. Overhead, fat white clouds hung like cotton puffs in a pale blue sky, while closer to earth a yellow butterfly rested on a meadow flower.

"Hey," she called, "you're going to shrivel up like a prune and then I won't love you anymore."

"Why? Don't you think prunes are sexy?" he responded from the stream. "Come on in and let's shrivel up together."

"Nope. I'm too lazy. You'll have to come to me."

She turned on her side and propped her head in her hand, watching her husband's lean grace as he waded from the gurgling stream. She never tired of watching him, his movements so sure, so masculine, and so beautiful. Her world was complete and she wished for nothing more, except . . .

It would be a frightening commitment, but the thought no longer petrified her as it once had. A baby. Could she do it? She was beginning to think she could, and should. He never mentioned it and though the thought occasionally crossed his mind, he never made her feel guilty or inadequate because of her decision. But she was stronger now, more in touch with herself. She thought she was ready.

He shook the water out of his hair, spraying it along her length, before pulling on his jeans; then he looked at her and caught her smile. "Enjoying the show?" he asked with a grin.

"Oh, it's all right. But you could use a little more practice on the bump and grind."

He threw back his head in laughter, his tall perfect body, shirtless under the summer sun, glistening and warm. He was tanned down to the line of his low-fitting jeans.

Remembering, she closed her eyes in a prayer of thankfulness.

A shadow blocked the heat from her face; she opened her eyes to find him standing over her. "What are you thinking?" he asked.

"That I want you to love me; that I want us to
 baby."

"I think that can be arranged," he said, dropping to his knees beside her.

Much later, he touched her beloved face. "Now what are you thinking?"

"That I've come a long way from Dallas."

He kissed her. "Was it worth the trip?"

She smiled, thinking of the road they had traveled and all the rough miles they still had to go. Then she reached for him.

"Oh, yes," she whispered, "it was worth it."

JOHN FARRIS

"America's premier novelist of terror. When he turns it on, nobody does it better."   —Stephen King

"Farris is a giant of contemporary horror!"
                                             —Peter Straub

Ramsey Campbell

☐	51652-4	DARK COMPANIONS	$3.50
	51653-2	Canada	$3.95
☐	51654-0	THE DOLL WHO ATE HIS	$3.50
	51655-9	MOTHER Canada	$3.95
☐	51658-3	THE FACE THAT MUST DIE	$3.95
	51659-1	Canada	$4.95
☐	51650-8	INCARNATE	$3.95
	51651-6	Canada	$4.50
☐	58125-3	THE NAMELESS	$3.50
	58126-1	Canada	$3.95
☐	51656-7	OBSESSION	$3.95
	51657-5	Canada	$4.95

Buy them at your local bookstore or use this handy coupon:
Clip and mail this page with your order

TOR BOOKS—Reader Service Dept.
49 W. 24 Street, 9th Floor, New York, NY 10010

Please send me the book(s) I have checked above. I am enclosing
$_____ (please add $1.00 to cover postage and handling).
Send check or money order only—no cash or C.O.D.'s.

Mr./Mrs./Miss _____
Address _____
_____ State/Zip _____
-llow six weeks for delivery. Prices subject to change